DEATH MAKES THE SCENE

No one seemed to know very much about the insignificant Barbara Jayne. When Matthew Furnival is lured to London to rescue his brother-in-law, caught red-handed with her naked, strangled body, he is out of his depth. But, assisted by Nicky, his willing but none too bright nephew, and Landseer, the discredited veteran sleuth, and romantically confused by Dinah, the gorgeous discotheque dancer, he sticks with it. Finally, he uncovers the evil behind the lively façade of the Birdcage Club.

Books by Stella Phillips
in the Linford Mystery Library:

DOWN TO DEATH
DEATH IN ARCADY
THE HIDDEN WRATH
DEATH IN SHEEP'S CLOTHING
DEAR BROTHER, HERE DEPARTED
YET SHE MUST DIE

STELLA PHILLIPS

DEATH MAKES THE SCENE

Complete and Unabridged

LINFORD
Leicester

First published in Great Britain in 1970

First Linford Edition
published 2002

British Library CIP Data

Phillips, Stella
    Death makes the scene.—Large print ed.—
Linford mystery library
    1. Detective and mystery stories
    2. Large type books
    I. Title
    823.9'14 [F]

    ISBN 0–7089–9795–3

Published by
F. A. Thorpe (Publishing)
Anstey, Leicestershire

Set by Words & Graphics Ltd.
Anstey, Leicestershire
Printed and bound in Great Britain by
T. J. International Ltd., Padstow, Cornwall

This book is printed on acid-free paper

1

Matthew Furnival glanced at the sign-post, and then at his wife seated beside him. Her face was pale and set, and her body strained tensely forward as though it was urging on the car.

'Ten miles to Reading,' he said casually. 'What about some lunch?'

'Oh, no, Matthew!' Joanna's voice was sharp. 'We mustn't stop! I've never known Elaine sound so urgent. It may be a matter of life and death.'

'But there's never much chance of being decently fed at your sister's — even when she isn't inarticulate with hysteria.'

'How can you be so callous when she's in such trouble.'

'We don't know what trouble she's in — she omitted to tell us. And I haven't had any breakfast.'

'You could scarcely expect me to get breakfast after the telegram.'

Furnival fairly conceded this. He

attempted to dispel his hunger pangs by thinking again about Elaine's extraordinary telegram.

They had just come downstairs — an hour later than usual as he had a few days holiday — when it arrived. It was addressed to Joanna, and he had taken it to her in the kitchen. Together they had read the curious message half-a-dozen times.

Come at once. Need Matthew. Great trouble. Gerald about to be arrested for m. of m. Elaine.

The urgency was typical of his sister-in-law, she lived in the imperative tense. Come at once, Indians attacking the fort! She didn't know that he was on leave; as far as she was concerned he could jettison the Meddenham police force and the case of a lifetime to run at her beck. And she did exaggerate, a similar telegram might have arrived if her poodle had been stolen — apart from that incredible last sentence. All they could be sure of was that she was in some sort of

2

trouble and would welcome the presence of her sister and brother-in-law who also happened to be a detective inspector.

Furnival and Joanna had discussed the telegram in bewilderment while the telegraph boy shuffled his feet in the doorway. Furnival *was* on leave, they had nothing planned — they *could* go. And much as he detested Elaine, her husband, her son, their London flat, and their whole tiresome set, he had to admit that if her telegram was designed to intrigue him it had certainly succeeded.

In the end they had composed an answer that combined drama, reassurance and economy.

Coming at once. Furnival.

Breakfast had been mutually forgotten in the rush of packing, closing up the house, and leaving essential messages. And conjecture had been postponed until he had manoeuvred the car through Meddenham's diabolic traffic.

Furnival had never been very familiar

with his sister-in-law. She had been long settled into London life when he had met and married her ten years younger sister, and there had not been a lot of contact since. When they were first married, Elaine, while pretending to find her sister's choice of a detective for a husband somewhat bizarre, had been secretly intrigued, hoping for macabre details and gruesome revelations to enliven her dinner parties, but Matthew's insistence on leaving his work at the office, and what she considered his infuriating discretion had soon quenched her interest. For his part Furnival found Elaine's frantic flitting from one interest and one acquaintance to another shallow and exhausting.

Of Gerald Harrington, his brother-in-law, he knew even less. He was around fifty-five, ten years older than Elaine. He was a stockbroker, and held one or two minor directorships. He had always seemed to Furnival a pompous self-satisfied man, and not a little stupid as he plodded along in the wake of his dragonfly of a wife. But he was utterly respectable and deadeningly conventional. His only two interests in life were the financial pages of the Times and his golf. Now if it had been Nicky, their only child, who was in trouble! Nicky, nineteen years old, and spoiled and indulged in everything by his parents, that was altogether a more likely situation.

Furnival came back to the present with a jerk.

'It must be Nicky,' he said aloud.

Joanna looked at him coldly.

'What do you mean, it must be Nicky?'

'It must be Nicky who's in trouble. Elaine must have made a mistake in the telegram.'

'Why should it be Nicky? You've always been down on him, Matthew, just because he enjoys life and goes round with a lot of exciting creative people.'

'I've never known one of them actually create anything. I should call most of Nicky's friends the freeloaders of society. When is he thinking of finding a job anyway? It's over a year since he was chucked out of that college.'

'He wasn't chucked out, the course

didn't suit him. He's looking around. Gerald can afford to keep him, he doesn't have to jump into the first thing that comes along. You're out-of-date, Matthew, things are different now, finding your feet — collecting experience, it's all regarded as a part of education.'

'I expect you're right, darling. I didn't mean to criticize,' Furnival knew he could never dent Joanna's loyalty to her family. 'I only meant that he seems a lot more likely than Gerald.'

'Oh, I don't know,' said Joanna vaguely. 'Gerald could have made a mistake over money. Misappropriation or something.'

'About to be arrested for m. of m.' mused Furnival. 'I suppose that could be it. Misappropriation of money, misplacement, mishandling. Are those crimes? I don't know. I hope Elaine isn't pinning her faith on me for any financial wizardry. You know my arithmetic stops when I run out of fingers.'

He noticed a coffee-bar in a new arcade of shops and pulled up in front of it, ignoring Joanna's irritated glance. Inside the café was clean, cold and deserted. He bought two cups of coffee and a couple of world-weary sausage rolls, and sat down beside Joanna at a glass-topped table. Joanna pushed the proffered sausage roll away and lit a cigarette, inhaling tensely.

'Why on earth did she make the telegram so cryptic,' she said.

'Had visions of hundreds of beady little eyes reading it all the way from London to Meddenham, I expect.'

Why Elaine had not telephoned was simple. Furnival had recently moved to a new house, and, despite the priority of his job, was still awaiting a telephone. He had a sudden vision of her, chic, skinny, sophisticated, ringing their old number, antagonizing the operator, ringing his office and no doubt mystifying Sergeant King, before rushing off to compose her telegram.

Furnival swallowed the last of his coffee and began to muse aloud again on Elaine's message.

'Mismanagement of money, of marriage, of mate! Misplacement of mind!' He began to feel rather lightheaded. 'Malice, mischief, malfeasance. Lovely word, malfeasance, almost worth committing it. Miching mallecho — '

Joanna stubbed out her cigarette angrily.

'For God's sake, stop being so idiotic, Matthew. Can't you see I'm sick with worry? You're so — objective. You treat it like a crossword puzzle.'

'All we've got so far is a crossword puzzle. But I'm sorry, darling, it's just that it's so difficult to think of anything really affecting Elaine.'

Joanna stood up abruptly, and Furnival followed her out to the car with a suitably contrite expression. It was early in May, the sky was cloudless blue and the sun was brilliant.

Traffic began to build up as they approached London, and he concentrated on threading in and out of the stream of vehicles. It was a particular intensity in Joanna that made his suddenly turn and look at her. She was leaning back against her seat, her eyes closed and her small face white.

'Not *murder*?' she said very quietly.

All at once there was an icy silence in

the car, in the passing traffic, in the gusty wind. It was as though everything was holding its breath. The words jumped into Furnival's head with absolute certainty.

'For murder of mistress,' he said.

'Mistress!' Characteristically seizing on the more heinous word, Joanna sat up abruptly. 'You must be mad! Gerald is nearly sixty. He's a company director!'

'Gerald is fifty-five — not quite past it. And I've never heard that company directors were exempt from the urge. Why should Elaine holler for me if it wasn't murder? My few murder cases are the only ones she's shown the slightest interest in, never the misdemeanours I spend most of my time toiling over. What use would I be if it was embezzlement? Gerald has an accountant, and a lawyer. Although what help I can be even if it is murder I can't imagine. I can't interfere, she must know that.'

'She'll expect you to investigate and discover the real murderer.'

'Joanna, I'm not Sherlock Holmes! Police work just isn't like that. The divisional police, the Metropolitan Police,

I suppose it will be in this case, will have all the evidence and all the witnesses' statements. They won't allow me to poke in.'

'But you could *talk* to people. Oh, but it's absurd discussing it in a void like this. We've no idea what has really happened. Why should it be a mistress, anyway?'

'What else? 'Murder of mother'? Or perhaps 'Murder of mate'? No, it couldn't be that — she sent the telegram.'

'You're being flippant again.' Joanna fidgetted restlessly in her seat for a moment. 'Surely you could overtake that lorry.'

'I could if I was tired of life.'

They fell silent. Furnival wondered just what sort of a mess Gerald had got himself into. Although he had not heard of any previous entanglements, he could not share Joanna's confidence in her brother-in-law's immunity. The man must often feel neglected by his wife's frenzied search for fulfilment. Any woman with the inclination could have added his scalp to her belt. Why any woman should feel such an urge was more of a mystery. Gerald seemed to Furnival a crashing bore and quite unattractive, in addition to which he was well into middle age and hardly wealthy enough to make it worthwhile. After Elaine had extracted the maximum alimony, which she certainly would, there would only be sufficient left for the most modest second establishment.

It was a mystery. Perhaps Gerald, with the foolish indulgence he had squandered on his son since the day he was born, had killed someone whom Nicky had got entangled with. But no, murder and Gerald simply did not go together in any possible context.

The traffic was now very heavy and he decided, for safety's sake, to give it his whole attention.

2

It was nearly one o'clock when they drew up in front of the block of flats where Gerald and Elaine lived. The Harrington's moved their abode fairly frequently, and, in Furnival's opinion, rather pointlessly, as each block of flats, so enthusiastically recommended by some new friend, seemed almost identical with the one before. This one, Manorleigh Court, in Joliphant Gardens, was fairly typical, a neo-Georgian white block of pleasant proportions, with green louvred shutters, and a glass sun lounge running along half of the front. There was a row of garages at the back, and a large gravelled forecourt with a couple of white painted wrought iron benches lurking among some handsome, miraculously unlopped, chestnuts.

Furnival stopped the car outside the porch and followed Joanna into the foyer. They waited for a moment before an elderly hall porter appeared from a cubicle in the corner.

'I'm calling on Mr Gerald Harrington,' said Furnival.

'Oh, yes.' The man leered knowingly. 'Been a lot of people after Mr Harrington. Number seven, first floor. Not worth you taking the lift, it's out of order anyway. Want any luggage took up?'

'No, thanks, not yet. I don't know whether we'll be staying.' They mounted the red carpeted stairs, Furnival hoping fervently that his in-laws would not have room to put them up. The occasional weekends he had spent with them in the past were not experiences he had any wish to repeat.

They reached the top of the staircase, and had not started along the passage that faced them, when a door at the end of it opened a few inches and Elaine Harrington peeped out.

Matthew Furnival was shocked at his sister-in-law's appearance. She had never, while he had known her, had a surplus ounce of flesh, but now the tiny bird-like bones seemed to push through her skin. Her great dark eyes ringed with bruised circles stared from her pale pointed little face, and her short black hair, always so fashionably cut, looked lifeless. She wore a gold quilted dressing-gown and no make-up.

She gave a shriek when she saw them, and ran to Joanna embracing her eagerly.

'Oh, Joanna, darling! Thank God you've come. We're in such a ghastly mess!'

Furnival firmly propelled the two women inside the flat and closed the door. They went through a tiny hall into a large, smartly furnished, but very untidy sitting-room. He pushed Elaine down into an easy chair, and he and Joanna sat on a settee facing her.

'Now shoot, Elaine,' he demanded. 'Let's hear what on earth this is all about.'

Elaine dried her eyes on a scrap of handkerchief and tried to rise from the chair.

'Let me get you something to eat first, after your long drive. Some coffee, at least?'

'Afterwards,' said Furnival. 'Will you please put us in the picture?'

Elaine fiddled with her handkerchief and stared at the tip of her feathery mules. It struck Furnival that it was the first time that he had ever seen her at a loss for words.

'Well, really, I hardly know where to begin — it's been such a shock. It's all so — unbelievable.'

'*Is* Gerald under arrest?' asked Joanna.

'No, at least I don't think so. But they've taken him for questioning. He was with the police for simply hours last night, assisting them in their enquiries they called it. They let him go at midnight, and we sat up all night talking it over. I tried to ring you from six o'clock on, where on earth were you? Then I sent my telegram, and soon after, about nine o'clock, the police came and took Gerald away again — for further questioning they said. He's still there now.'

'But, darling, what for?' broke in Joanna. 'What's it all about?'

'I told you. For murder.'

'*Murder?* But that's absurd! Gerald, of all people. It must be some sort of mistake.'

Elaine turned on her sister. 'Well, of course, it's a mistake. You don't think he did it, do you? I've rung up lots of people we know, important people — a magistrate, J.P.'s, but they all say they can't interfere. You'd think people would rally round at a time like this! You were our last resort.'

'Elaine,' said Furnival gently. 'It does sound as though they have fairly strong evidence against Gerald. Did he tell you what had happened. Who was murdered, anyway?'

'Oh, a girl. Some young girl. Gerald barely knew her.'

'In your telegram you said he might be arrested for m. of m. What did you mean?' Furnival delicately omitted his earlier surmise. 'Was M. her initial?'

'No,' Elaine plucked at the handkerchief some more. 'I meant for murder of mistress. That's what the police are trying to make out it was. It was a sort of shorthand. I thought it would fetch you. I don't know if Gerald even knew her name.'

'Hardly likely to be a mistress then. She

could have been a casual pick-up, of course. Do you believe Gerald when he says he barely knew her?'

'Yes, I do,' said Elaine firmly. 'I wouldn't swear that Gerald has never had a mistress, or even that he hasn't one now, in fact I think there is someone. We're sophisticated people, we live our own lives, and I've been so busy with my boutique lately. Did I tell you, Joanna, I've opened a darling little boutique up West. It's doing frightfully well.'

'Elaine,' said Furnival slowly. 'I think you've lost me. Are you saying that, after all, this girl might have been his mistress?'

'No, no! Do try to be less dense, Matthew, you're getting to be an absolute hick. I said Gerald could be playing around, but not with this girl.'

'Why not? What was the matter with her?'

'Well, for one thing she was very young, not more than eighteen. Gerald wouldn't take a girl as young as that around, it would have made him look ridiculous. And she was such an ordinary little thing, no personality at all. Really she was just — nothing.'

'Poor little devil,' murmured Furnival. 'It hardly seems worth being born. Eighteen years of being nothing, and then getting yourself rubbed out at the end of it.'

'Don't be sentimental,' said Joanna. 'It's Gerald you're supposed to be helping. The chances are the girl was a little better than a prostitute anyway. Probably killed by one of her clients.'

'No, I don't think she was that,' said Elaine. 'I didn't mean to sound callous but — well — Gerald has become accustomed to some sophistication and style, and I doubt if this girl had much of those.'

'Where did he meet her?'

'She was his manicurist.'

'His what?'

'She did his nails. At Gino's. Gerald has found this awfully good little hairdresser over in Linden Terrace. This girl started working there about six months ago. I've seen her once or twice when I've picked Gerald up there, but I can barely remember her. As I say she was very insignificant.'

'Did Gerald know her apart from that?'

'No I'm sure he didn't.'

'But you say he might have a girl-friend?'

'I believe he does see someone occasionally. I'm out a lot in the evenings, and several times lately he's been out when I've got back.'

'But didn't you ask him about it?' demanded Joanna.

'No, I didn't ask him,' said Elaine slowly. 'I suppose I didn't want to know for sure. I enjoy my life, it's very — comfortable. I didn't want to be involved in any boring, soul-searching scenes.'

'How does Gerald come to be implicated?' Furnival pressed. 'Was he with the girl when it happened? Did he find the body? Where was she killed, anyway?'

'She was killed in her flat. She had a room in a house in Avery Street, quite near Gino's shop. Gerald was implicated because he was found with her body. She was naked.'

Furnival's eyes shot open. Old Gerald was revealing quite unexpected hidden depths. 'How was she killed?' he asked.

Elaine choked and looked sick, her mouth started to tremble. Joanna went across and knelt beside her sister, putting her arms around her shoulders.

'That's enough, Matthew, she's had enough. I'm going to take her to lie down. Gerald can answer your questions when he gets back.'

'If he gets back!' moaned Elaine. She shrugged off Joanna's arm. 'I'm all right. She was strangled, Matthew.'

Strangled. The word lay between them in the pleasant room with an almost tangible evil. An ugly, obscene word with nothing chic or sophisticated about it. There was a long pause. It looks bad, Furnival thought. It looks about as bad as can be.

'Where is Nicky?' he asked.

'He went off yesterday morning for a couple of days with two friends. He should be back sometime today. He doesn't know anything about this yet.' Elaine's eyes welled with tears. 'It's going to be the most horrible shock for him.'

'Now Elaine,' Furnival tried to put a confidence into his tone that he did not quite feel. 'I expect Gerald will be home at any moment completely cleared. The girl may have been dead for hours, and Gerald could have an alibi for the time.'

'No.' Gerald Harrington had come quietly in at the door and was leaning wearily against it. His normally ruddy face was pale with exhaustion and shock. 'No, they say she had just died, not more than ten minutes before they found me with her,' he said.

3

'The police doctor said she had only been dead a very short time. And in any case she was seen alive only twenty minutes before by the old busybody in the basement flat.'

They were sitting around the lunch counter in the Harringtons' smart red leather dinette. Joanna had persuaded Elaine to dress and do her face, and she was beginning to enjoy her role of injured, but loyal, wife. Matthew and Gerald had prepared coffee and sandwiches. Already the atmosphere was a little less distraught.

'Where was she seen?' asked Furnival.

'Entering the house.'

'Alone?'

'Yes.'

'What sort of girl was she?'

'I hardly knew her,' said Gerald. 'I saw her half-a-dozen times when she did my nails and we used to chat. She was a friendly little thing but there was something slightly pathetic about her.'

'Was she pretty?' demanded Joanna.

'She was a bit colourless, but, yes, when she made the effort she could look very pretty.'

'So you did see her away from work!' Elaine pounced.

'No, I didn't. I didn't mean that. I meant that sometimes she looked rather scruffy, her hair unkempt, no make-up, that sort of thing. She seemed to neglect herself.'

'I wouldn't have thought Gino would have put up with that,' said Elaine. 'He is always so immaculate — and the boys.'

'He used to scold her, but he was very good to her although she was unreliable, coming in late or not turning up at all. I think he felt sorry for her.'

'Could they have been having an affair?' asked Furnival.

'I don't think Gino cares for girls!'

'He's homosexual?'

'I don't know. He puts on the act. He isn't married and he always goes about

with young men, although he must be
nearly forty.'

'He could have had a sort of protective
attachment to the girl, I believe it
happens. Who else is employed at the
shop?'

'Two young men, Terry and John.'

'Did either of them appear to have a
special relationship with the girl?'

'No. I think they resented Gino
favouring her.'

Furnival took a sip of coffee from a
mug resembling a hollowed-out log and
about as comfortable to drink from. 'I
honestly don't see what I can do,' he said
reluctantly. 'It's in the hands of the police,
I can't interfere.'

'But you did at Brinwood,' broke in
Joanna. 'When you were staying in that
caravan. You were on holiday, it was
nothing to do with you, but you took over
from the local man and solved the whole
thing.'

'That was very different. I was right in
the middle of it before it happened. I
found the bodies. I knew all the people
involved. Here I can't do anything except

lend moral support, and perhaps interpret the police's moves for you. But don't worry, Gerald, they're very thorough. You won't be arrested for anything you didn't do!'

'Of course I'll be arrested!' moaned Gerald. 'They think they've got a watertight case. I don't blame them. Good God, I was practically caught red-handed.'

'Yes, how did you come to be there?'

Gerald shuffled sheepishly. 'I was going to see a friend. She has a room in the same house as Barbara. That was the girl's name, incidentally — Barbara. Anyway, I went up to my friend's room — it was exactly eight o'clock — and there was Barbara dead on the floor, naked except for a little silky kimono.'

'In your friend's room?'

'Yes.'

'Where are the two rooms? Near to each other.'

'Yes, both on the first floor, off a small hall. No one else lived on that floor.'

'And your friend presumably wasn't there?'

'No, I didn't expect her for a few minutes. I was to wait'
'Was the door locked?'
'No, just closed.'
'What did you do?'
'I panicked.' Harrington shuddered at the recollection. 'I didn't know she had been murdered, of course, but dead, and with no clothes on! I simply couldn't be found in that position. I thought if I could put her back in her own room and slip away it would be the best thing.'
'You knew which was her room?'
'Yes, my friend had told me she lived there. Well, I started to drag her across the hall when suddenly the old woman from the basement flat appeared on the staircase and started to yell bloody murder!' He ran his hands distractedly through his thinning sandy hair, ruining Gino's no doubt expensive efforts. 'I tried to shut her up, but that made her worse. She thought I was attacking her! The noise she was making brought the landlady up from the ground floor. *She* took one look and dashed back down to phone the police. When they arrived they

took me in for questioning.'

'Not unreasonably,' murmured Furnival. 'Did your friend turn up while all this was going on?'

'No, she must have been held up.'

'She probably killed the girl and made off leaving you to carry the can.' Elaine's smile was venomous. 'They've probably been fighting over you for months, dear.'

'Elaine, why don't you come to the bedroom and lie down,' said Joanna diplomatically. 'You must be quite exhausted, and the men can talk more freely without us.'

'I'll bet they can,' snapped Elaine. 'But I think I'm entitled to know the extent of my husband's stupidity. And I must be here to break it to Nicky when he comes in, it's going to be quite shattering for him.'

'Nonsense,' said Furnival brutally. 'If I know Nicky he'll be dining out on it for months.'

'Well, you don't know Nicky, Matthew. He's an extremely sensitive boy.'

'Could we keep to the point?' begged Furnival.

'I think Joanna is right, Elaine. Gerald and I will be able to talk better alone.'

Elaine was escorted, still reluctant, into the bedroom by Joanna, having extracted a promise that she would be roused the moment her child returned.

When the women had gone there was a long silence between the two men.

'I don't know about you,' said Gerald finally, 'but I'm going to have a drink.'

'It's a bit early for me,' said Furnival, 'but O.K. — under the circumstances.'

'And let's get off these bloody stools,' went on Gerald ' — they're giving me piles.'

He fetched a bottle of Scotch and two glasses from a kitchen cupboard, and the men returned to the living-room and settled into easy chairs.

'It's a hell of a mess, isn't it?' said Gerald.

'It is. Frankly, I'm surprised they didn't charge you last night.'

'Perhaps it was my attitude,' said Gerald. 'I think they could see I was genuinely bewildered by everything.'

'There would have to be something

more than that — they see some damned good actors. You say she had only just been killed?'

'Yes, they told me that several times. The doctor said she hadn't been dead more than half-an-hour when he saw her. That meant only ten minutes before I found her.'

'I suppose you didn't see anyone else hanging around?'

'No, not a soul. But this old bag from the basement told the police that she saw me creeping up the front steps five minutes before.'

'Did she see anyone else go up?'

'No, and I don't suppose she misses much. Just my luck she missed him.'

'He must have left within seconds of you arriving.'

'Well, I didn't see anyone,' repeated Gerald. 'I was too concerned with not being seen myself. Anyway, he might not *have* left. He may live in the house. Have you thought of that?'

'Yes, I had. Any ideas who does live there?'

'There's the old woman in the

basement, Mrs Cobbett she's called. Then the owners, the Marshalls, have all the ground floor. Then there was Barbara and my friend on the first floor, and two more tenants on the second floor. One of those is a coloured girl, I don't know who the other is.'

'It doesn't sound too hopeful, apart, perhaps, from this unknown.' Furnival fixed his brother-in-law with what he hoped was a penetrating gaze. 'Look here, Gerald, this 'friend' of yours does exist, I suppose? If it was really Barbara you were going to see, for God's sake tell me now.'

Gerald goggled. 'Does exist? Of course she exists. Her name is Marian. We've been going out for nearly a year. I'm very attached to her.'

'O.K. I believe you. How long had she lived at this house?'

'Only a month. I got the flat for her. She was living at home with her parents which was a bit — well — awkward for us. She was delighted to get a place of her own. As a matter of fact, Gino put me on to the flat. I expect he got Barbara fixed up there, too.'

'Proper little live wire your Gino. What is he, a house agent on the side?'

'He knows everybody — they tell him when they're changing flats — you've got to be in the know in London.'

'Did the girls come with the flats?'

Gerald's always ruddy complexion suffused with anger. 'Are you suggesting he was pimping for the girls? I assure you there was nothing of that sort at all. I didn't pay him for putting me on to the flat. I might recommend his shop to friends, but that's all. That's the way these things are done. I can't speak for Barbara, but Marian is a very respectable girl. She's a private secretary. Good heavens, her father is a retired army officer!'

Furnival accepted these irreproachable references looking noticeably unimpressed. 'You're going to have to produce her, you know,' he said.

'I'm not having her dragged into it.'

'The police will pick her up as soon as she goes back to her flat.'

'They haven't found her yet. I'm hoping she has heard what has happened and moved back home.'

'Well, I'm not. For God's sake don't try to be noble, Gerald. If your Marian can't be found the police are going to be convinced it was Barbara you set up in a flat.'

'The other people in the house will have seen Marian. Her stuff will be in her flat.'

'But it doesn't connect her with you. Unless she comes forward and says that you were in that room at that time for the purpose of meeting her, the implication is that you were visiting Barbara. Gino found you the flat, Barbara was his employee, he doesn't even know Marian.' He paused. 'I wonder which flat she was killed in. Did you notice whether the room was disturbed?'

'She was killed where she was found — in Marian's room. The police told me that. Was the room disturbed?' Gerald thought, and gulped his whisky. 'I was in such a flap I wasn't noticing much. I can tell you my knees turned to water when I saw that poor kid on the floor. But, no, I don't remember any signs of disturbance. The rugs scuffed up — that was all.'

'What about Barbara's own room? Did you get a look at that when you were moving the body?'

'Only a glance. I'd just opened the door when the old woman started screaming. It was very untidy, but just normally untidy, I should say, not as the result of a struggle.'

'I wonder why she was in the wrong room,' mused Furnival. 'If she was killed there presumably she got there of her own volition. Do you think she'd been drinking?'

'She didn't smell of drink.'

'Did she ever flirt with you at the shop? Did you get the impression she was inviting a pass?'

'She was one of those girls who wouldn't know any other way to act with men. They appear to give you the come on with their manner and their skirts up to their behinds, but if you took them up on it half of them would scream rape.' He stood up, staggering a little either from fatigue or the three whiskies he had rapidly consumed.

'Can't you do anything, Matthew?' he

begged. 'I know we've never been particularly close, but for Elaine's sake — '

Furnival stifled an inclination to retort that he had never been particularly close to Elaine either.

'What did you have in mind?' he asked.

'I thought you might have a word with the detective in charge. He's called Calvert. He seems as though he might be a decent chap if one met him in different circumstances. And then you might make a few enquiries at Gino's, and at the house.'

'No,' said Furnival firmly. 'That's quite out of the question. I'd go and have a word with Calvert, if you like, although he'll probably show me the door — I couldn't blame him if he did. But I'm not butting into the investigation. Don't worry, if he knows his job he'll be looking very thoroughly into the girl's background.'

'Why should he bother to look any further,' Gerald muttered. He broke off, staring at Furnival in alarm as quick light footsteps advanced down the corridor and the outer door to the apartment was opened. Then the living-room door burst open and Nicky Harrington posed in the entrance, resplendent in a tan suit and primrose silk shirt.

He laughed when he saw his father's expression. 'Don't worry, Dad, it's not the fuzz coming to take you in! But what *have* you been up to? I just called in at Gino's and the joint is fairly jumping. They say you're up to your eyes in your actual *crime passionel*!'

Matthew Furnival stifled his usual feeling of extreme repugnance at the sight of his nephew and rose to his feet, his hand extended.

Nicky Harrington was in every way his mother's son, small boned and slight, graceful in movement and gesture, with large dark eyes, fine brows, and dark feathery hair. He would have made an extremely pretty girl, and, contemporary taste being what it is, he did all right as a man. He was idle, vivacious and irrepressibly frivolous.

'Don't talk in that bloody stupid fashion!' yelped his father. 'It's a hell-of-a-mess. Your mother is in a terrible state.'

'O.K. keep your cool!' Nicky perched on a chair arm and swung an elegant foot. 'Have we not a super sleuth in the family come roaring 'oop from t'country' to the rescue.' His rather prominent dark eyes flicked mockingly over Furnival.

'Not much I can do, I'm afraid, Nicky. And your father isn't exaggerating. He's got himself into a nasty hole.'

'Cheer up,' retorted Nicky. 'They can't hang you for having a bit on the side!'

'It mustn't come to trial,' groaned Gerald. 'It would ruin my business — and our social life. It would kill your mother.'

'Isn't Uncle Matthew going to rally round then?'

'He can't interfere, Nicky.'

'Not much point in having a cop in the family, is there? Oh well, I shall just have to ferret around and see what I can dig up for myself.'

'Did you know the girl?' asked Furnival.

'I saw her around the shop, that was all. Very provincial little thing. How would you go about it, Uncle Matthew, if you *were* in going to investigate?'

'I'd enlarge her circle of acquaintances,' said Furnival. 'We know that Gino employed her, his male assistants resented her, you and your father had noticed her about. No one can make as little impact on life as that. But I do advise you to leave it to the police, Nicky.'

'I know — they're doing a wonderful job! But don't worry about me getting into trouble — if you were. I've just had a rather bright idea.' He ambled to the door. 'See you later!'

'Wait!' called Gerald. 'Hadn't you better go in to see your mother?' But the light footsteps were tripping down the hall.

Gerald looked at Furnival apologetically. 'He's at a difficult age,' he said. 'They can't bear to show their feelings, but I could tell he was upset.'

'Yes,' said Furnival doubtfully. He stood up. 'Look, if I'm going to see this bloke Calvert, I'd better get it over with. Where do I find him?'

Gerald gave him directions to the

police station where he had been held for questioning. 'Thanks a lot, Matthew. Should I come with you?'

'No, better not. I'll get back as soon as I can.'

Furnival went slowly down the stairs and across the foyer. He did not at all relish the chore ahead of him. He imagined that already two or three people turned to look at him as he passed.

4

Furnival found the police station with little difficulty. It was a newish, red-brick building standing on what was probably a cleared bomb-site, among a conglomeration of shabby houses and small shops and cafés.

He crossed the entrance hall to a long glassed-in counter where an elderly desk sergeant was writing up a report book, and a young cadet listened attentively on the end of a telephone. The sergeant finished his paragraph, carefully restored his pen to the tray, and looked at Furnival over his spectacles.

'I'd like to see Superintendent Calvert.'

'He's out at present, sir. Will anyone else do?'

'I don't think so. It's in connection with the Avery Street case. I believe Superintendent Calvert is working on it?'

'That's right, sir. Do you wish to give information on the matter?'

'No, no, I — I'm Detective-Inspector Furnival from the Meddenham C.I.D. My brother-in-law, Gerald Harrington, has been — helping with enquiries.'

'I see, sir.' The man gave Furnival a long, hard stare that spoke volumes. 'Well, as you'll realize the superintendent is very busy just now.'

'Is he here?'

'No, I think he's at the scene-of-crime at the moment.'

'Do you expect him back?'

'I believe he meant to call in again.'

'Then I'll wait if I may.' Furnival looked around and seated himself on a wooden bench against the far wall of the room. He could understand the sergeant's coolness. He had suffered himself on many cases from the interference of friends and relatives, all insistent on the innocence and uniquely noble character of his suspect.

He had been waiting for twenty minutes when the swing doors crashed open and a small group of men erupted into the room. In the lead talking loudly was a man whom Furnival felt instantly sure would be Calvert. He was very tall, and well — almost too well-dressed. He had a high-cheek-boned face, with bright sardonic dark eyes, raking black eyebrows, a hawk-like nose and rather long curling black hair. He was about thirty-five years old.

Three other men of comparatively ordinary appearance hurried in his wake.

'Superintendent Calvert,' said the desk sergeant. 'Gentleman here to see you.'

Calvert stopped in his tracks and looked down at Furnival from his great height. 'Does it have to be me? I'm damned busy.'

Furnival stood up. He wasn't used to looking up to people but Calvert cleared his own six feet by four or five inches. 'I realize that,' he said. 'I shan't keep you long. Detective-Inspector Furnival.'

'Oh.' Calvert stared at him. He pushed open the door nearest to them. 'Well, come in,' he said abruptly. The three other men hesitated in the doorway. Calvert turned to the nearest, a plump balding man. 'Give us ten minutes, Pritchard.'

He followed Furnival into his office and dropped into the chair behind the littered desk.

'This is rather mystifying, Inspector. What can I do for you?'

'What I expect you to do is chuck me out,' said Furnival apologetically. 'Gerald Harrington is my brother-in-law.'

Calvert raised one expressive eyebrow and waited politely.

'Well,' Furnival struggled on. 'Naturally they — that is, he and his wife — are horrified, not to say scared, at his involvement in this business.'

'Mr Furnival,' broke in Calvert. 'I can do without interfering relatives just at the moment.'

'They've got the wind up. They imagine Gerald is on the point of being arrested.'

'He was found with the girl's body right after she died. What am I supposed to need?'

'Not a thing, I should say,' said Furnival unhappily.

'You have an excellent case.' He started to rise. 'I'm sorry to have barged in like this, but my wife and my sister-in-law won't believe that my being in the Force can't be utilized somehow. I realize you can't confer with me, but I had to go through the motions. I don't even know whether or not Gerald would be capable of this, we don't usually know our in-laws all that well, but I swear it was a fantastic shock.'

'It usually is,' said Calvert. He extracted a slim gold cigar case from his pocket, offered a cigar to Furnival which was refused, and lit one for himself. 'There's one thing your brother-in-law should be thankful for. I am a very careful man. It *is* an excellent case, but I'm not going to move until it's one hundred per cent watertight.'

Furnival sat down again. 'Is there anyone else in the running?' he asked. 'A boy-friend, perhaps?'

'We haven't been able to find out much about the girl. We can't trace where she came from or her next-of-kin. She called herself Barbara Jayne but that's obviously phoney. Gino, her employer, knew her previous address but it was only digs where she had stayed for a very short time. He says she drifted into his shop about six months ago and asked for a job. After a couple of weeks she told him she was unhappy in her digs and he got her fixed up with a flat at the Marshalls. He also says she wasn't very reliable or good at her job, but he kept her on because she had a pleasant manner and the customers liked her. He didn't pay her very much. He doesn't know of any friends that she had, and neither do the two laddies who work for him.'

'What about the people at the house, did they notice her callers? My brother-in-law says there is an old woman who doesn't miss much.'

'She doesn't, but unfortunately last night she was out in the backyard tending to some flower tubs for about a quarter of an hour before she saw Harrington go in. She went out to the yard immediately after she had noticed Barbara come home. For the fifteen minutes between the two anyone could have gone in or out. She notices the regular callers, she remembers seeing Harrington twice before, but, of course, she doesn't know

44

which rooms they visit. She suspects most of them go to the top floor where there is a coloured girl who's 'no better than she should be'. The Marshalls — they own the house — are out all day, and they don't seem to be interested in anything that goes on, except collecting the rent.'

'What about the woman whose room Barbara was killed in?'

'Harrington's *petite amie*? Well, she exists. At least a woman has lived there for the past month. She calls herself Miss Smith, you'll be amazed to hear. Very quiet and respectable, according to Mrs Marshall.'

'That sounds more like Gerald.'

'There's nothing to link her with him. He could have noticed her previously, and pretended in the heat of the moment that it was her he was visiting.'

'A bit too quick thinking for Gerald. In any case, he *was* in her room.'

'Well, she hasn't put in an appearance yet and neither have the two from the top floor, the coloured girl, and the young man who has the other flat. I shan't do anything definite about Harrington until

45

they all come home to roost and I can interview them. If they don't come home, we must go out and find them.' Calvert leaned back in his chair and regarded Furnival through a haze of cigar smoke.

'Anything else you'd like to know?' he asked sardonically.

Furnival recognized a man with a need to think aloud and decided to chance his luck.

'Have you the medical report on her?' he asked.

'Yes.'

'Was she pregnant?'

'No, she wasn't.'

'A virgin?'

'You must be joking. I expect she lost that commodity before she left school. She'd been aborted fairly recently. Quite a neat job the pathologist says, although probably not done by a doctor.'

'Poor little devil. I suppose she was a prostitute?'

'They don't like the label, they haven't the professional pride of your old-fashioned whore. They're models, or club hostesses nowadays. One other thing

— she was a junkie. She was on heroin.' Calvert unlocked his desk drawer, took out the case file, and selected a document. He tossed it across to Furnival. 'Here's the medical report. You might as well have a look at it.'

Furnival read through the detailed report and then turned to the photographs. There were a dozen close up and full length shots from every angle. He saw a small girl, who may once have been pretty, sprawled in an abandoned position on a carpeted floor, her flimsy robe open, her careful dignity gone. Long straight fair hair streamed around her head. She looked very young. Pity and anger rose in him.

He passed the report back to Calvert. 'There wasn't much violence used,' he said. 'Minimal bruising and laceration.'

'No, they didn't knock her about much. No sexual assault, either. It's the one odd feature in a very commonplace case. A rather unstable young girl drifts up to London, no family connections, takes a flat on her own, gets into bad company, gets herself killed by a boy-friend. It happens every day. But the killing was unusual. There had been a struggle before she died but it wasn't a life-and-death struggle. I can only call it a gentle struggle. The man could have been trying to persuade her to do something, but not to have sexual relations with him. There wasn't that sort of drive.'

'You said she was on drugs,' said Furnival. 'I think that was in the back of my mind. Gerald said that she was frequently late for work or didn't turn up, and that she was sometimes 'scruffy and unkempt', so drugs were a possibility. Surely that widens the scope of the enquiry? A girl mixed up in a drug racket could have any number of reasons for being murdered.'

'A drug racket?' Calvert's long mobile mouth lifted in amusement. 'Just what exactly do you know about illicit drugs, Mr Furnival?'

'I went to a lecture once,' began Furnival.

'You went to a lecture once! And you have a lot of colourful boyhood memories of Fu Manchu and wily oriental villains! There is no criminal underworld of drug traffickers in Britain. Every piece of British legislation has been designed to avoid the American situation, where punitve measures have led to large scale addiction and all the attendant crime that brings. In the U.K. there is provision for the addict to obtain his drugs legally and at a low cost. Why should the gangs move in? There's no market. There's no economic incentive.'

'And everything in the garden is rosy? Oh, come off it!' said Furnival. 'I'm not quite such a bumpkin as that. I only have to read my newspaper to know that arrests are made for illicit drug trafficking every week.'

'That's a different sort of thing entirely, unless you're talking about cannabis, and I assume you're not. There's plenty of trafficking of the sort you mean in 'pot'. With heroin and morphine there is only a kind of black market among addicts, they'll sell part of their prescription to a fellow addict for rent or food money. They'll alter prescriptions, or steal prescription forms from doctors surgeries and forge them. There have been thefts of small amounts of drugs from chemists shops and hospitals. But it's all on a small scale, and it's all among addicts. No one is exploiting them — yet.'

'But I don't understand. If addicts can obtain their drug supply as cheaply and legally as you say, why do they need to resort to illegal methods at all. Why the forging and pilfering?'

'It is a bit more complex than I've made it out to be,' agreed Calvert. 'Remember we're not dealing with people whose reasoning is functioning very well. To begin with a large number of addicts will not register as such. They don't want their families or their employers to know, they imagine it will stay on their records, and a number have the odd conviction that they're not really 'hooked' until they register. A more real fear is that they will be forced to take a cure.'

'But there is a big increase in addiction?'

'Yes, an alarming one, and addicts are much younger than they used to be. But that isn't the doing of any vice ring. It's because there are a lot of bored affluent kids about who have tried hash, and taken every sort of pill until they rattle, and who are eager for new kicks. Also Britain's more permissive attitude brought a lot of American and Canadian addicts over here. And there's no doubt about it the over-prescribing of a few doctors in the past created new addicts. That's why it was taken out of their hands and the new treatment centres were set up. It's a statutory offence now for a doctor who is not on the staff of a treatment centre to prescribe heroin or cocaine to addicts.'

'But an illegal market *could* be built up,' pressed Furnival. 'If a man was evil enough and greedy enough, and had the outlets. Look, Barbara wasn't raped, there was no unnecessary brutality — might not that argue an impersonal act? A business murder by a gang?'

'No, they would have made a bigger mess of her — they enjoy their work! I really think we can discount gangs, Furnival, this isn't Chicago or the Shanghai waterfront. The only relevance Barbara's drug addiction has is that addicts are very much more prone to meet violent deaths than normal people. Their suicide rate is fifty times as high! But I can fit Harrington into the picture quite neatly. One, Barbara was his mistress and was teasing him, or holding out on him, or threatening to tell his wife. There is a struggle as a result of which she dies, but years of gentlemanly breeding inhibit him from really roughing her up the way a young yob would. Or, two, we accept his story, he barely knows Barbara, but he had a mistress established across the hall, and while he was waiting for her Barbara came in and made a pass at him. She was hard up, and here was the nice, friendly, generous man she manicured right on the spot. Harrington is appalled,' continued Calvert, warming to his reconstruction. 'He and Miss Smith have been so discreet, no naked teenage nymphos for him. He can't get rid of her, he's terrified of his wife finding out, and, worldly as she is, I think she would have drawn the line at Barbara. Perhaps he's also frightened of his mistress, whom he may be genuinely in love with, misunderstanding the situation. He tries to evict Barbara, and, possibly accidentally, strangles her. He panics and tries to get her back to her own room. Now that version,' said Calvert, smiling like a satisfied cat, 'I really like!'

There was a long pause. 'I suppose it couldn't have been done by a woman?' said Furnival. 'That ass couldn't be covering up for his mistress?'

'Do women have that sort of restrained scrap? I would have expected more scratching and smashing of ornaments. And they rarely strangle, although, of course, it's not impossible.'

'What about hand dimensions? Finger-prints on skin?'

'The lab are working out the handspan, it appears to be rather small,' said Calvert. 'There were no fingerprints — gloves were worn.'

'And Gerald, I assume, was wearing gloves?'

'He was.' Calvert got to his feet and held out his hand to Furnival. 'So that's how it stands at the moment. We'll try to fill out the girl's background, find out who her friends were, and look into the drug angle. We'll leave no stone unturned, as the saying goes, but, and I'm sorry to have to say this, I think it will all be a waste of time.'

Furnival thanked Calvert for his time, and made for the door. As he reached it Calvert called his name, and turning he saw that the amiable smile had disappeared. 'Furnival, I don't have to tell you not to go prowling round the scene-of-crime, or attempt to question my witnesses, or anything of that sort. I wouldn't take kindly to that at all.'

Furnival walked down the corridor and out of the building feeling very depressed. Calvert thought Gerald was guilty, and Calvert had all the facts before him and was palpably no fool. He reached his car and waited while a trio of police cars jostled out of the gate, all busy, all intent on some well-defined task. He felt lost and helpless, he had no bearings in this area. He did not know where the murder flat was, nor Gino's. He wasn't even very sure of his way back to Elaine's! He certainly didn't know anything about drug trafficking in London, or, he thought ruefully, anywhere else.

He turned the car out of the narrow crowded street, found the main stream of traffic, and, after a couple of false turns, located Joliphant Gardens. He turned into the forecourt of Manorleigh Court and immediately spotted two curiously ill-matched figures seated on one of the benches under the chestnut trees. As Furnival stepped out of his car Nicky Harrington rose and beckoned conspiratorially to him. Furnival approached the seat.

'I'm glad you've come, Uncle Matt,' whispered Nicky. He indicated his companion. 'I couldn't have kept him here much longer, and I didn't want to take him up to the flat. Dad probably wouldn't approve.'

Furnival looked down at the other man. He didn't seem reluctant to stay. He puffed contentedly at his pipe, gazing away into space as though glad to be taking the weight off his feet. He was a man of about sixty years of age, tall and heavily built, but badly run to fat. His face was a mottled red, and a fringe of greasy grey hair protruded beneath a greasy grey hat. His eyes were small, blue, and somewhat watery, and his nose was as round as a little dumpling. He wore an ancient navy blue pin-striped suit with trousers wide enough to accommodate an extra leg.

The man caught Furnival's look and without word or expression raised the hat an inch to reveal a band of white unweathered skin before firmly resettling it on his head.

'Who is it?' murmured Furnival.

'It's Landseer,' said Nicky. 'Landseer, the detective.'

'The *what?*'

'The detective. I thought we might employ him.'

'*Employ him?* Are you out of your mind?'

'Well, I know he doesn't look like much, but I thought he might be a sort of front for you.'

'What is that supposed to mean?'

'You've been to see Calvert, haven't

you? And there's nothing doing. Landseer knows him, and he says that bastard would never let you go poking in.'

'He's quite within his rights.'

'Oh, quite, but that doesn't help Dad. But there's nothing in the world to prevent anyone employing a private detective. Landseer could go around interviewing people, asking questions you'd prepared for him, and you could deduce from them. Oh, come on, Uncle Matt, we could give it a try! He doesn't get much work.'

'You surprise me!'

'He's had a lot of experience,' persisted Nicky. 'He was on the Force in this division for twenty years. He finished up as detective-sergeant. Honest, Uncle Matt, he's not nearly as dim as he looks and he knows just everybody.'

A faint spark of interest kindled in Furnival. Landseer looked a feeble reed to pin any hopes on, but twenty years in the Force must count for something. He could at least speak to the man, it would be uncivil not to. Besides Nicky's enthusiasm was infinitely more appealing than his usual pose of blasé decadence. He crossed to the silent figure.

'Mr Landseer, I'm pleased to meet you. I expect my nephew has wasted your time bringing you here. I don't think there's any way you can help us.'

The man showed no signs of relinquishing his seat, but smiled up at Furnival comfortably.

'Don't write me off too soon, Mr Furnival. I know this neighbourhood like the back of my hand.'

Furnival sat down. 'Did you know the murdered girl?'

'I don't know. How could I? There are so many of them and they all look much alike. But give me three hours and I can bring you a dozen people who did.'

'Do they think she was on drugs?' he went on.

Furnival started. 'Why do you ask?'

'Drug addicts seem to be prone to violent death. Stands to reason a young girl could get herself killed if she stumbled on to anything. There's some very nasty characters operating in these parts, Mr Furnival, you'd be surprised.

This is the third kid who has died suddenly in the past six months.'

'But if this sort of thing is rife, why should Calvert fasten on to my father?' interrupted Nicky. 'Doesn't he know about it?'

'Certainly he knows about it, and don't you worry, he'll look into these gentlemen's whereabouts very thoroughly.'

'Gangsters!' breathed Nicky.

'Well, yes, so you might call them.' Landseer rearranged his haunches more comfortably on the wrought iron. 'But they're not the sort of blokes for you to go messing with, young man. They play very rough.'

'What did you mean about Barbara being the third kid to die?' asked Furnival.

'Six months ago a young boy by the name of David Summers, was found dead in an alley not half-a-mile from here. And three months ago his girl-friend was found gassed in her room. They never decided whether that was an accident, suicide or murder. But I did hear they were both heroin addicts, so if your young lady was on the junk there could be a link.'

'Yes,' said Furnival. 'Ever hear of anyone pushing it in this area?'

Landseer smiled. 'Ah, you want a free sample.'

Furnival hesitated, there was something impressive about Landseer's quiet confidence.

'How is your standing with Superintendent Calvert?' he asked.

'Well, not too fragrant, I'll admit, Mr Furnival.'

'Mm, a pity. Still, I don't see it will do much harm to try to ferret out some people Barbara was friendly with. But for God's sake don't get in the way of the police.'

Landseer heaved himself to his feet. 'Don't worry about that. I'm just as anxious to keep off their toes as you are.'

He crunched heavily away across the shingle watched by Furnival and his nephew.

'What about you, Uncle Matt?' asked Nicky. 'What are you going to do?'

'I,' said Furnival, 'am going to get my hair cut.'

5

Furnival decided to take Nicky along to Gino's with him to effect the introductions. They went up to the Harrington flat for a few minutes, where they found Gerald, Elaine and Joanna sitting around looking like the last survivors of a dying planet. Furnival gave them a brief run-down on his actions so far, staved off their eager questions, and begged them, with disconcerting success, not to pin too much hope on him.

He went down to his car again, followed eagerly by Nicky, and found his way to the Edgware Road where the traffic had just passed the rush hour peak.

'Where to now?' he asked.

'Linden Terrace. Second right and first left, it's only half-a-mile. He'll be closed, though, it's half-past-six.'

'Pity. I'd have liked to have seen his face when I asked for a short back and sides! Think he'll still be there?'

'I expect so. He lives above the shop.'

They drove on in silence while Furnival negotiated the unfamiliar streets.

'Here we are,' said Nicky after a few minutes. 'Pull over to that meter.'

Furnival parked the car, got out, and looked back at Gino's establishment. It occupied the basement of a small, beautifully maintained terrace house. The railings and handrail of the steps down into the area were painted brilliant white. The area itself had been paved with different hued flagstones, and was set about with potted trees and wrought iron benches. The entire wall of the basement floor had been replaced with a bottle glass bow window and door. Inside the window Furnival could see several pounds worth of red roses. Above the door a small, tasteful sign read *Gino's*.

'Very attractive,' he said, 'and pricey.'

'Yes,' agreed Nicky. 'He's doing very well, everyone comes here. We sit out here to wait in good weather. Proper little club it is.'

Furnival tried the door which was locked, then rattled it gently. From a booth down at the dim rear of the shop a figure emerged and wavered towards them, looking, through the distorted glass, like some exotic tropical fish viewed through its bowl. The young man opened the door and regarded them enquiringly. He was small and slender, with golden hair cut to hug his head like a helmet, round china blue eyes, and a small mouth. He wore a smock of peach-coloured nylon.

'Nicky, darling,' he squealed to that young man. 'You've just caught me, I was on the point of toddling off. How awful about poor Mr Harrington, it's absolutely ghastly for both of you.' He turned the big blue eyes on Furnival. 'Oh, my God, have the police got you too, Nicky?'

'This is my uncle,' said Nicky.

'Lord, I'm sorry, I really am,' burbled the young man. 'I'm quite *contrite*, but you do look like the fuzz you know, darling.'

'He is a policeman,' said Nicky. 'But not here, out in the backwoods somewhere. He's on holiday.'

'A policeman *and* your uncle, how

quaint! Well, come in, darlings. Gino's through in the back if you want to see him, although the poor old dear is quite shattered. I'm John, incidentally.'

'How do you do?' said Furnival heavily. He looked around the interior of the shop. It was totally unlike Tom's, his own barber in Meddenham High Street. It was more like one of the high-class female establishments where he occasionally escorted Joanna. The leather chairs, bowls, dryers, and towels, were all in matching tones of lavender and lilac, and there was a deep dove-grey carpet on the floor. Myriads of flasks and bottles of coloured liquids glittered in the dim light and were reflected in the many mirrors. There was an overwhelming scent of expensive perfumes on the air.

There was a little fluttery eruption from a curtained booth and a second young man joined them. He was the other side of John's coin, like him young, slight and exquisite, but with dark hair and eyes, wearing a lemon-coloured smock.

'Naughty John,' he chided. 'Keeping company to yourself.'

'I thought you'd gone,' said John sulkily.

'Just combing out my set, darling. Why, it's Nicky back again. And who is this lovely gentleman?'

'This is my Uncle Matthew,' said Nicky. He had the grace to look abashed at the behaviour of the two creatures. 'This is Terry, Uncle Matt.'

Furnival nodded briefly, keeping his hands firmly in his pockets. 'Is Gino here?' he said. 'I'd like a word with him.'

'Oh, isn't he cute?' trilled John. ' "I'd like a word with him". Just like a policeman! Yes, he is here, but, I told you, he's very upset about Barbara getting herself killed.'

'He was fond of her?'

'My dear, she could do no wrong! It made you sick.' Terry pouted his rosy lips. 'Gino can be an absolute bitch to John and me when he's in a tizz, but Barbara, she was rotten at her job and she was always late, but he'd just take it all and never say a word.'

'Except over the see-through blouse,' giggled John. 'Don't you remember, when they were in fashion, and Barbara bought one and wore it to work? I thought Gino was going to throw a fit.'

'Not good for trade?' asked Furnival.

'With our clientele? You must be joking! Scare the pants off most of them. Anyway, he made her change right away, and he put the blouse in the waste bin.'

'Very proprietorial,' said Furnival. 'Could he have been having an affair with her?'

'Oh gawd, no. Nothing like that.'

'Are you quite sure.' Furnival hesitated delicately. 'Doesn't he care for women?'

'He isn't queer, if that's what you're getting at. He puts on an act to make the boys feel at home, but it wouldn't fool anyone. He's had plenty of girl-friends, but, of course, he wouldn't like it to get about.'

'Of course not,' agreed Furnival gravely. 'But Barbara wasn't one of them?'

'I'm sure she wasn't. She was his employee, and she was too young, and there just wasn't anything, anyway.' John smugly regarded his reflection, segmented in a dozen mirrors. 'I would have known

— I'm awfully sensitive over relationships.'

'Did you know anything of her personal
life? Where she went? Who she was
friendly with?'

'She didn't know *anybody*, dear. And
she didn't seem to go anywhere much. In
fact, I never saw her outside of work, did
you, Terry?'

'God, no,' said Terry. 'And wouldn't
want to. Really Matthew, she was nothing
but a little amateur tart.'

'*No, she wasn't*. Don't talk like that
about her!' A door at the back of the
salon had opened quietly and a man
stood in the doorway.

Twenty years ago he must have borne a
strong resemblance to Terry. He, too, was
small and still slender, with glossy dark
hair and large brown eyes, but his grace
of movement had stiffened, and in some
odd way he had thickened without
fattening. His eyes were a little puffy
beneath, and there were faint crow's feet
at the corners. Two deep lines were
etched from his nose to the corners of his
mouth. At first glance he would have

passed for an Italian, but his tan had the slightly unnatural tinge of a sun-ray lamp, and his voice was utterly English. He looked deeply agitated now, holding the side of the doorway and glaring at Terry with bright dry eyes.

'I'm sorry, Gino, I really am,' said Terry. 'I shouldn't have gone on like that. Me and my big mouth!' He took Gino's arm and led him forward like a child. 'You know Nicky Harrington — you gave him those super Sable Highlights last week. Well, this is his Uncle Matthew, and he's a pet, and he wants to have a little chat with you. John and I are just toddling. *Come on, John.*'

'Well, let me get me smock off!' grumbled John. 'Can't walk down Linden Terrace in this.' He shrugged into a lilac cashmere cardigan and waved a graceful hand. 'Bye, bye, everyone!'

The two young men passed through the front door and went fluting up the area steps. Gino rubbed his hand across his temples, disturbing his immaculate hair.

'Will you come into the back?' he said

heavily. 'Or upstairs to my apartment?'

'The back will be fine,' said Furnival.

With Nicky he followed Gino down a short passage to a small, brightly-lit room behind the salon. It contained a desk with a swivel chair behind it, a filing cabinet, an assortment of drying hoods, and a couple of shabby fireside chairs. Against another wall a small kitchen table held a gas ring, a large homely brown teapot and half-a-dozen plain white mugs. Gino lifted a pile of glossy photographs of last week's hair styles from the swivel chair and slumped into it. He looked up at Furnival.

'I'm sorry about Mr Harrington's predicament. The boys tell me the police think he was involved in Barbara's death.'

'They certainly do, he's got himself into quite a mess. I'm trying to find out something that might help him.'

'Are you a lawyer, Mr Furnival?'

'No, I'm a police inspector, but I don't work in the Metropolitan area. In fact I've no more right to be questioning you than any ordinary member of the public.'

'But we want to get Dad out of it,'

interrupted Nicky.

'Your father hasn't been arrested, has he?'

'Not yet, but he may well be,' said Furnival.

'But why? I understand he was at Barbara's house. What was he doing there?'

'Apparently he has a woman friend established there.'

'Of course, I remember now. I helped him get the flat for her. I've never met her.'

'Well, he was visiting her last night. When he got to her room he found Barbara's dead body on the floor. He was trying to return her to her own room when he was spotted.'

'Hasn't he an alibi for the actual time of the killing?'

'It more or less *was* the actual time of the killing, or only a very few minutes after.'

'We've been trying to discover any friends she might have had,' put in Nicky, 'but we haven't had much luck.'

'I don't think she had many friends.

She was new around here, it's hard to make friends in London, particularly for a young girl.'

'I would have thought it was easy,' said Furnival. 'She was very pretty.'

'You mean casual pick-ups? No she wasn't that type of girl.'

'So what did she do after work every night? Go straight back to her room to read?' Furnival's tone was doubtful. 'Don't you think she'd have tried to tap the life of the big city?'

Gino gathered up the glossy photographs on his desk and began to stack them fussily into a tidy pile. 'I'm sorry, but I can't help you at all. I advise you to leave it to the official police. Tell your father to get himself a good lawyer, Nicky.'

Furnival walked round to the front of the desk and perched on the edge.

'Was she a bad girl, Gino?' he said.

'No! I told you she wasn't.' The little man's eyes came up fiercely. 'She was — indiscreet. I had to speak to her once or twice about her manner with the customers. She simply didn't realize what a jungle London could be for a young girl on her own.'

'How do you mean, her manner with the customers? Was she soliciting them?'

'No! What sort of a place do you think this is? She was flirtatious, but there was no bad in her. She was just trying to make friends. It was pathetic.' To Furnival's discomfiture Gino's eyes filled with tears. 'She was like a friendly puppy.'

'She'd had an abortion.'

There was a long pause. Gino took out a bright silk handkerchief and blew his nose.

'You know that?' he said. 'Do the police know?'

'Oh, they'll know everything like that. They won't know about her being lost or lonely, or a pathetic little puppy looking for a friend. But anything like that they know.'

'She told me,' said Gino. 'She told me everything.'

'When was it done?'

'About a year ago, just after she came to London. That was why she came.'

'Who was the man?'

'She never said.' Gino spread his slender bejewelled hands. 'He didn't matter, he was just a boy.'

'Where did Barbara come from?'

'Originally? I've no idea. She was in digs out at Wembley before she came here. I gave the police the address. But she didn't feel she was really in London; she wanted to move nearer to the heart of things.'

'You say she told you everything,' said Furnival. 'You haven't come up with much so far.'

'She didn't tell me those sort of things — not matters of fact. But she talked for hours about her hopes and her dreams. She was a great one for dreams. She wanted to be a model, but she was too small. She was very keen to be a pop singer — she occasionally sang with the groups who play at the clubs around here. She had a pretty little voice, but she didn't seem to put across much personality. She wanted an exciting life — '

'And she wasn't in any way qualified for it. I know the type, they pour into

London in droves. So you don't know any of her friends, or anywhere she went?'

'I believe she went to some of the clubs and discotheques around here, when she could find someone to take her,' said Gino reluctantly. 'They're not suitable places for a young girl, and she stayed out much too late. I've often had to speak to her about it.' He sounded staid and old-fashioned. 'I suspected she was keeping bad company.'

'What about drugs, Gino?' Nicky interrupted. 'Do you think she was on drugs?'

'No, I'm sure she wasn't.'

'But she was,' said Furnival. 'She was on heroin. The police know that, too. Do you have any idea where she might have got it?'

'Of course I haven't!'

'Oh, come off it!' burst out Nicky. 'You hear people talking in here, you must get to know that sort of thing. Don't they ask you if you know any place?'

'No, they don't. And if they did I should tell them to get out. I hate drugs, filthy, filthy stuff — destroying young people, mere children, before they've even begun their lives.' Gino broke off abruptly and covered his face with his hands.

He did love her, thought Furnival. In some way — his own way — he loved her. 'Will you help me?' he said. 'Help me to clear my brother-in-law?'

Gino took his hands from his face. 'I wouldn't try to clear anyone who had killed her,' he said.

'Of course not. I wouldn't ask that. But this background of drug pushing opens it up. Gerald had nothing to do with that sort of world. There could well be somebody else. You say you hate these people who supply drugs to kids. Maybe they caused her death. Maybe we could uncover them.'

Gino stood up wearily and looked at Furnival.

'What do you want me to do?' he asked.

'First, take me to her house,' said Furnival.

<h1 style="text-align:center">6</h1>

The house where Barbara had lived and died was less than half-a-mile from Gino's shop, and Furnival, getting his bearings, began to realize that he was operating in a fairly small area. He mounted the steps with Gino, Nicky having left them to keep a previous engagement, and rang the bell. As they waited he looked over into the area and saw the lace curtain at the basement window twitch.

The door was opened by a woman in her fifties, with a hard face, and a hair-do that looked as though it had been created in an expensive foundry.

When she saw Gino her mouth tightened.

'Well, Gino, a nice sort of tenant you found for me! Getting herself murdered — and in the nude, too. I've had six reporters round here already, and photographers taking pictures all over the place;

to say nothing of the police prowling about half the night asking endless questions. I wish to God I'd never rented to that girl. I could see she was no good the minute I set eyes on her. Dirty little bitch!'

'May we come in, Mrs. Marshall?' interrupted Furnival, seeing the pain in Gino's eyes.

The woman moved aside reluctantly and let them into the hall.

'Who are you? More police, I suppose?'

'My name is Furnival. It was my brother-in-law who found the body.'

The woman laughed harshly.

'Found the body that's good, that is! He'd just murdered her, the swine, although I expect she asked for it. A man of that age carrying on with a mere kid — it's disgusting!'

She opened the door of a large sitting-room at the front of the house. 'I never wanted the bother of tenants, anyway. We were going to do the house up into separate flats and resell it for a nice profit. There's big money in conversion nowadays. We got the place cheap because there was a sitting tenant. The old woman was at least seventy, and she was supposed to be dying on her feet — '

'Mrs. Cobbett?' interposed Furnival.

'Yes, but she's no nearer snuffing it than she was when we bought the house.' Her face assumed an expression of intense self-pity. 'It was supposed to be an investment, but we've had nothing but trouble with them all from the beginning.'

'Had Barbara given you any trouble?'

'Well, no,' said the woman reluctantly. 'I can't say she had — until now. She was very quiet, she hardly ever had anyone in.'

'Do you know of anyone who visited her?'

'No, I don't. I don't take much notice of them. I'm out at work all day. As long as they pay their rent and don't cause any trouble, I ignore them.'

'How much rent did you charge Barbara?'

'Eight guineas a week.'

'Did she pay it herself?'

'Of course she paid it herself.'

'Did she ever chat to you? When she paid her rent, for instance?'

'She'd try to strike up a conversation. She was quite a friendly little thing. But I don't have the time. Anyway, as I told you, the tenants are just an investment. I don't want to be involved in their problems.'

Poor little Barbara, thought Furnival. What a friendly home-away-from-home you found. 'Tell me about your other tenants,' he said.

'I told you about the Cobbett woman downstairs. On the first floor, across the hall from Barbara's room, there's another young lady. The one Harrington claims he was calling on.'

'What is she like?'

'Oh, she's a very nice lady, a model tenant. Very quiet and respectable, pays her rent on the dot. Marian Smith, she calls herself on her rent book.'

'And on the top floor?'

'On the top floor there's a young man who has one room. The two bigger rooms are let to a coloured girl, a dancer or something. She's a bit of a nuisance. She has a lot of people up there, late at night sometimes, but I get a very good rent off her, so I don't want to get rid of her if I can avoid it.'

'Tell me about last night, Mrs. Marshall?' said Furnival. 'Was anyone else in the house at the time, except you and Mrs. Cobbett?'

The woman stuck a cigarette into a short holder and dragged on it. 'Not that I know of. I'd only been in an hour myself, I'd just finished my evening meal in the back. Rob and Dinah, that's the two on the top floor, weren't in, and neither was Miss Smith. In fact, Rob and Miss Smith haven't come back yet. My husband has been away all week at a conference.'

'And you didn't see or hear anyone else in the house?'

'No. But then I wouldn't at the back of the house. The walls are thick and I had the radio on. All of a sudden I heard Mrs. Cobbett screeching. I didn't take any notice at first, I thought she was having a row with someone. I thought, 'What is that old witch doing upstairs' Then I went up myself and saw what was going on.'

'What did you see?' It was the first time

Gino had spoken. He sat, small and neat, on the edge of his chair. His voice was barely audible.

Mrs. Marshall turned to him. 'I saw this Mr. Harrington dragging Barbara across the hall. Mrs. Cobbett was screaming, and he was pushing her away and pleading with her. I wasn't frightened at first, I thought the girl was drunk and they were just larking about. I couldn't take it in. Then he lowered her to the floor and said, very politely, 'I'm afraid she's dead, Mrs. Marshall.' So I went downstairs and rang for the police.'

'Have you ever seen Harrington here before?' Furnival asked.

'Yes, I noticed him once coming up the steps.'

'With Miss Smith?'

'No, alone. I've no idea which of the girls he visited.'

Mrs. Marshall stood up and smoothed her twin-set over her bosom. 'I really think I've talked to you long enough, Mr. Furnival. I just didn't know anything about the girl. I don't suppose I said more than fifty words to her all told.'

Furnival stood up. 'Thank you for giving me so much of your time, Mrs. Marshall. I'd like to talk to Mrs. Cobbett. And to the girl on the top floor if she is home.'

Mrs. Marshall reluctantly agreed, and the two men returned to the hall where Gino left to return to his shop. Furnival descended to the lower regions in search of Mrs. Cobbett. As he had expected, she was awaiting his arrival, her living-room door wide open.

Furnival tapped on the door and was invited to enter. Mrs. Cobbett was sitting in a basket chair near the window where he surmised she spent a large part of her time. She was tiny, thin, and very wrinkled, but still managed to suggest a tenacious hold on life. She wore a draped lavender creation and amber beads; her sparse grey hair was arranged in bangs over her forehead. Two enormous cats blinked up at Furnival from her feet.

'More police, is it?' she asked eagerly as Furnival entered. 'My word, what handsome men they're recruiting in the Force these days! Your Mr. Calvert is a very charming man.'

'I hope you won't mind telling your story again to me, Mrs. Cobbett,' said Furnival carefully avoiding laying any claim to Mr. Calvert. 'I'm from a different department.'

'Not at all. I think it does me good to talk about it — gets it out of me system. Draw up a chair, dear.

'In all the years I've lived in this house I've never known such a shocking thing,' she went on. 'Do you know how long I've lived in this house, sir? Thirty-nine years. Those Marshalls upstairs can't wait for me to shuffle off. The house doubles its value, you see, if they can get rid of me. But I'm not going yet. I was telling her last week what a long-lived family we are — my mother lived to be ninety-seven. She went quite green!' The old woman cackled with laughter.

'Mrs. Marshall doesn't seem to notice much that goes on in the house,' suggested Furnival.

'Turns a blind eye, you mean,' said Mrs. Cobbett promptly. 'Just as long as she gets her money, that's all she cares. I've told her countless times, the house will get a bad name the way she lets them all carry on.'

The larger of the two cats landed with a thud on Furnival's knees and started to knead them enthusiastically.

'He likes you,' said Mrs. Cobbett with approval.

'Do the tenants have many visitors?'

'Tramp, tramp, tramp up the stairs all evening sometimes.'

'Did Barbara Jayne have many visitors?'

'That the one who was murdered? No, I can't say she did. In fact she looked rather a nice little thing — only a kid. No, most of the callers went on up to the second floor, and I'll tell you how I know. The stairs are only carpeted to the first floor, and I can hear people clattering on up the wooden stairs. A lot of young people go up to see that noisy young man, and a lot of men call on the darkie. She's no better than she should be — man mad they are, you know, dear.'

'But no callers at the first floor?' pressed Furnival ignoring this fascinating gambit. 'What about the man who came here with me tonight? The one who has just left?'

'Little pansy bloke? No, I've never seen him before. I've seen the murderer twice before, though. *He* stopped at the first floor.'

'Do you know which girl he visited? Barbara or Marian Smith?'

'Is that the new lady on the first? Well, I suppose he visited Barbara. Stands to reason, doesn't it? It was her he murdered. And that new one looks quite a respectable girl. It's funny, but I was just beginning to think we were getting a better class of tenant.'

'Did this man visit before Miss Smith arrived?'

'I didn't notice him until recently, but I'm not prying out of the window all the time.'

'So you don't know of anyone else who visited on the first floor except my — except the murderer?'

'No I don't. But I'll tell you one thing — that young man on the top floor used to go down to her a lot. I heard him clattering up and down all the time.'

'To Barbara?'

'Must have been. The new woman is ten years older than him. In any case, he used to go before she came.'

Furnival tickled the cat's neck and it began to purr deafeningly. 'Thank you, Mrs. Cobbett,' he said. 'You've been very helpful. Now I'd like to run through the actual murder with you if it wouldn't distress you too much.'

'I can stand it, sir. We had to be tough in the old days. I stayed here all through the blitz, you know. I can stand it if it will be a help to you.' It was obvious that this episode was now to be the outstanding event in Mrs. Cobbett's life, outdoing even the blitz and her two uniquely complicated childbirths.

'What exactly did you hear that made you go upstairs?' Furnival asked.

'I heard a furtive sort of thumping and dragging,' said Mrs. Cobbett promptly. 'I'd seen this chap creeping up the steps to the front door ten minutes before. It was the third time I'd seen him. A big well-dressed chap in his fifties, reddish

face and hair. He looked like a gentleman. Should have known better, I expect
he's got a nice little wife and family
somewhere.

'Anyway, I heard him go up to the first
floor and open a door — I don't know
which, then, a few minutes later, this
bumping. So I thought I'd better go up to
see what was going on. I crept up and
peeped round the bend of the stairs, and
the sight that met my eyes! My heart
dropped right to my shoes, sir.'

'Well?' prompted Furnival unnecessar-
ily.

'He was dragging the girl across the
hall. He had hold of her under the arms,
her heels were dragging, and her poor
little head was lolling on one side. She
had nothing on except a bit of a wrapper,
and it had fallen open and was showing
— well, everything.

'But it was the man's face that turned
my stomach. Terrifying, it was, with his
lips slathering, and his eyes rolling in his
head. He was mad with lust! I don't really
know what I did, but I must have run
towards him and tried to pull the girl

away, and I think I started to scream. He went for me like a madman. I thought my last hour had come. Then Mrs. Marshall arrived.'

'I think you were very courageous, Mrs. Cobbett,' said Furnival, not untruthfully. He evicted the cat from his knees and stood up. 'You say it was only ten minutes between when you saw the man on the front steps and when he was dragging Barbara's body across the hall. He didn't have a lot of time to kill her.'

'He had enough,' said Mrs. Cobbett firmly. 'If he just *leapt* on her.'

Furnival turned to go. If Mrs. Cobbett ever got into the witness box Gerald's goose was surely cooked. 'Thank you for your help,' he said. 'I'll go up to see the girl on the second floor now.'

'You want to watch yourself with her,' Mrs. Cobbett was sulky now that her moment was over. 'Proper man-eater, she is.'

Furnival made his way up from the basement, past the Marshall's apartments, and ascended to the first floor. He paused at the square hallway. It was blue-carpeted like the staircase, and four doors led off it. Two of them were locked and had police seals affixed to them; the third opened to reveal a big, old-fashioned bathroom. He slipped inside, but apart from the usual appointments and some towels, it was quite empty. The fourth door concealed a lavatory with a handsome mahogany seat and a flowered bowl.

He closed the door and proceeded on upstairs. The second staircase was, as Mrs. Cobbett had said, uncarpeted. On the second landing he was again faced with the choice of four doors and he was looking at them uncertainly when he heard low singing coming from behind one of them. He knocked on it, and a woman's voice invited him to enter.

The girl standing on the far side of the room turned to look at him as he came in. She was the colour of burnt honey, with great dark eyes and a full luscious mouth. Her straightened gleaming black hair was piled in a loose knot on top of her head. She was wearing a brief waist slip and a scrap of bra both in apricot satin, and high-heeled mules. She emphatically was not a girl you brought home to meet mother.

She smiled, lifting her short upper lip off dazzling teeth, reached slowly for the white towelling robe that lay on the bed, and wrapped it round herself.

'Do I know you, mister?'

'No. My name is Furnival. I'm making some enquiries into the murder of Barbara Jayne.'

'Who are you? A private detective?'

'You could call it that.'

The girl's eyes flicked over Furnival appraisingly. 'Not bad! I thought all private detectives were fat old retired cops with bunions.'

'That'll come.'

She laughed and dropped gracefully into a chair, looping her toes under another to drag it forward.

'Well, take the weight off them for a bit. Not that I can help you; I scarcely knew the kid.'

Her voice had a faintly transatlantic accent, but whether from birth, or because it was the accepted currency of

her world, he could not tell. He looked
about him. The coloured girl's room
was luxuriously furnished and carpeted.
Built-in wardrobes stretched the whole
length of one wall, and through their
open sliding doors bulged a lavish array
of clothes.

'Did you ever speak to Barbara,
Miss — ?' he asked.

'Miss Merriman, but call me Dinah.
Sure, we used to meet on the stairs and
chat a little. She was keen to get into
modelling and she seemed to think I
could help her.'

'Did you ever see her away from here?'

'No. I don't imagine our paths would
cross.'

'Did you know any of her friends?'

'No.'

'Ever introduce her to anybody?'

'No.'

'What was she like?'

'She was just a dim little thing. Very wet
behind the ears. She was always trying to
make the scene.'

'Would you say she was on drugs?'

The girl started, and her warm, lovely

face hardened slightly.

'How would I know. I don't suppose so. They certainly didn't do much for her if she was.'

'I don't imagine they do. I expect you get around, Miss Merriman, do you know of any place around here where she might obtain drugs?'

'I never heard of any. That's something I don't need.'

'But some people do — or imagine they do. People less self-sufficient, like Barbara. Are you sure you never saw her at a club or somewhere of that sort?'

'I told you, I'm quite sure.'

'O.K. What about last night?'

Dinah Merriman shook an American cigarette from a carton and lit it, inhaling deeply. Her robe fell aside revealing a length of smooth golden thigh. 'I can't help you about last night. I went out at six o'clock and I came home at three this morning. Mrs. Marshall told me what had happened at noon when I woke up.'

'Do you know the man the police have been questioning? Gerald Harrington, a big chap, about fifty-five, with reddish hair?'

'I don't know him. I think I've passed him on the stairs.'

'Who did he call on?'

'That woman who moved into the flat below, I imagine.'

'Not Barbara?'

'Hell, no! I can tell you the sort of mistress a man like that will choose. She'll be like his wife — a little prettier, a little younger, and a little bit kinder — but not too much of a change.'

'And how did this mystery woman measure up?'

'Well, I don't know his wife, but Marian Smith is about thirty; dark brown hair, blue eyes, not bad looking but with a kind of bossy disapproving look — like the girl in school who always cleaned the blackboard. About my height, but not so well stacked.'

Furnival regarded Miss Merriman's statistics without reluctance. Allowing for the high-heeled slippers she was about five feet six, and would have assayed out at about nine stones.

He got up to go. 'If you should think of anywhere you saw Barbara, or anyone you saw with her — '

'O.K., but don't hold your breath.' Miss Merriman stood up and with practised ease her robe opened a little at the front. 'Do you really have to go? How about a drink?'

Furnival made it to the door. 'Some other time, thanks, Miss Merriman.' He sped down the stairs, through the front door, and down the steps to the street. It was now entirely dark. A shadowy mass quietly detached itself from the area. Furnival spun round on the defensive, his mind flashing to beatings-up and vice in the capital. The figure raised its hand and lifted its hat an inch. 'Got a bit of a report to make if you're ready, Mr. Furnival,' said Landseer.

7

Furnival laughed shakily. 'How did you find me?'

'Saw your car. Thought you might be here.'

'Well, let's go and sit in it. If you've got anything at all to report you're a better man than I am. As far as I can see Barbara was a complete non-person. Nobody talked to her, nobody visited her, and she didn't go anywhere.' Furnival opened the car door and the two men sat in the front. Landseer lit a cigarette.

'She went to the Birdcage,' he said.

'The Birdcage? What's that?'

'It's a club. A discothèque as they call them. They're patronized by young people. They dance to records and beat groups, and drink, mostly soft drinks, but there's plenty of hard drinking done at the Birdcage. It's got a bad name, I heard rumours of drug pushing. Just pills and pot, nothing about heroin, that's regarded

as in a different class. But you remember
I told you that two other local youngsters
died recently? Well, they used to go there
a lot.'

'Where is it?'

'Over in Alder Court, not far away.'

'How did you find out Barbara went
there?'

'I hung around in the coffee bars near
her flat. In one place I met a couple of
girls who knew her slightly, and they said
they'd seen her at the Birdcage several
times.'

'Who was she with?'

'Once or twice she was alone, but
usually she was with a young man; always
the same one. Big, built like a rugger
player, in his early twenties. The girls
think he's an Australian.'

'Who runs this place?'

'He's known as Mr. Leslie. A very nasty
customer, although he's probably only the
front man. He drives a white Bristol.
Always seems to have plenty of money to
throw about.'

'Barbara had too much money as well,'
said Furnival. 'Her flat cost eight guineas

a week and Gino is reported not to have paid her very much.'

'He could be lying,' said Landseer. 'Perhaps she was blackmailing him — found out his real name was Alf Bloggs!'

Furnival laughed. 'He didn't seem to favour an investigation. I suppose he's afraid it would be bad for business.'

'That sort of thing wouldn't put his customers off — they'd go anywhere for kicks. But his shop could be an outlet for drugs — it would be ideal. Or maybe he's paying protection to Mr. Leslie and his bosses and doesn't want to collaborate in anything that might annoy them. He's got a nice place, he wouldn't want to have it wrecked.'

'Or maybe he isn't guilty of anything that concerns us,' said Furnival. 'Everybody thinks they've got something to hide, diddling their income tax, or a girl friend they want to keep quiet.' He looked at his watch. 'It's after eight, I'd better go back to the flat for a bite. I'll have a look at the Birdcage later, I don't suppose it will be hotting up yet. Oh, I forgot, I turned up a boyfriend of sorts, too. It seems the lad from the top floor used to descend to visit Barbara pretty regularly.'

'O.K., you can let me out here. I'll keep ferreting,' said Landseer, climbing heavily out of the car. He turned and leaned in at the window. 'I'm beginning to enjoy this job, Mr. Furnival. Maybe these kids who flock up to London ask for what they get, but the blokes who exploit them, they're the scum of the earth. They ought to be put down!'

He lumbered away, and Furnival turned the car towards Joliphant Gardens, deriving satisfaction from the fact that he was beginning to get his bearings.

In the flat Nicky was still out, but his wife and his in-laws were waiting to bombard him with questions. He staved them off, pointing out plaintively that he was starving, and they adjourned to the kitchen where Elaine unfroze a couple of chops.

'It doesn't look quite so hopeless,' he told them. 'The girl may well have stumbled into a semi-criminal world. She was known to frequent a club called the

Birdcage which has an unsavoury reputation. Two other youngsters who used to visit the place have died rather mysteriously in the last six months.'

'That sounds promising,' said Elaine. 'And we haven't heard anything more from the police, which must be a good sign. Are you going to the club, Matthew?'

'I thought I'd go after supper. Pity Nicky isn't here to come along with me.'

'I think he's snooping around on his own,' said Elaine. 'I hope the silly boy doesn't do anything reckless. But you can get into the Birdcage on your own, Matthew. Lots of middle-aged voyeurs go to these places for kicks.'

'What about the flat?' Gerald, looking very subdued in the corner spoke for the first time. 'Did you go to Avery Street?'

'I've just come from there.'

'Do tell us what you thought of Gerald's girl friend,' put in Elaine sweetly.

'She wasn't there,' said Furnival shortly. 'The chops are burning, Elaine.'

'Probably in the river!' muttered Elaine, bringing the chops to the table with buttered rolls and coffee. 'Overtaken with remorse!'

'I saw Mesdames Marshall and Cobbett, a formidable pair,' said Furnival. 'And a lovely coloured girl from the top floor. And I talked to Gino and his acolytes, but they didn't know much about Barbara. Nobody does, so it's to be hoped I can pick up a lead at this club.'

Furnival finished his supper and went into Nicky's bedroom where Joanna had left their suitcases. He examined the change of clothes he had brought, but there seemed to be nothing that would establish his *bona fides* at the Birdcage as a middle-aged voyeur or anything else. He settled for changing his shirt, attempted to brush his short hair forward over his forehead, thought better of it, and went down to the car.

Elaine had supplied directions to Alder Court, but it took him some time to locate the narrow street that ran between two busy thoroughfares. It was dimly lit, and was mainly composed of small shops and cafés, dark now and shuttered for the night. He had driven the length of the street twice before he noticed in a doorway an unobtrusive sign depicting a birdcage. He parked the car and walked back to the entrance. Furnival walked down a long, poorly lit passage to a second door through which he could hear the monotonous thump of a beat group. He pushed open the door and the noise increased. Before him were three steps leading down and a third door beside which a young man was lounging.

'Good evening,' said Furnival. 'My nephew is a member of the club. He was going to bring me tonight, but unfortunately — '

The youth rearranged his shoulder blades against the wall. 'Ten bob,' he said.

Furnival produced ten shillings, and the young man jerked his head at the door beside him. Furnival pushed it open and the blast of music at full amplification hit him like a bludgeon. The room was dark, lit only by flashing blobs of psychedelic light in various shades of pink and purple that writhed across the walls and ceiling like demented amoebae. When his eyes accustomed to the gloom he saw that the room was large and very crowded. The dance floor was packed and so were the chairs around the edge. On a dais at one end of the room four young men girt about with guitars and drums were in the last stages of frenzied possession. Eyes tight closed, mouths wide, their faces white and sweaty, they yelled incomprehensible words into the clamour of their instruments.

Furnival edged round the room to the spot farthest from the musicians and sat down. Nearly all of the company was very young, most had drinks in front of them, some cokes and minerals, but many hard drinks. There was a smell of perfume, sweat, cigarette smoke, and an unfamiliar acrid smell that interested Furnival very much.

The group stopped playing for a blissful moment and a young girl stepped up from the dancers, conferred for a moment with the lead guitarist, and was reluctantly handed the microphone. The music started again and the girl started to sing. She was very bad. Even this simple and unbeautiful sound was not quite so easily achieved as it appeared. People of Furnival's generation and background would have clapped the girl's pitiful efforts in sympathy for a sporting try, but these cruel young eyes froze her off the floor. She stepped from the dais, head down, and scuttled round the edge of the room. As she reached Furnival's table, the empty chair beside his was in her path. He smiled at her, trying to look honourable, upright and sober, and at the same time not too dull, and said, 'Won't you sit down? I enjoyed your singing.'

The girl flopped down in the chair. 'It was lousy, and you know it. Got a fag?'

Furnival gave her a cigarette, and she dragged on it moodily. She wore a skimpy wrap-around dress in black jersey, and ugly clumping shoes. Her make-up was freakish; her skin was polished gleaming, her lipstick was a zombie white, and her eyes were contoured in silver with black pencilled lines starring out from her lower lid. Her hair had been permed to a close cap of frizz. She looked about sixteen.

'It's the group,' she explained. 'The Zodiacs. They're rotten, but they think they're fantastic. Coming in at the wrong time, too loud, too fast.'

Furnival peered through the haze at the band. On the drum kit, in letters so artistically executed as to be almost unreadable, he could just make out the legend, the Zebra Zodiacs.

He grunted his sympathy. He was about to say, 'Do you come here often?' decided it was inadvisable and changed it to, 'Can we get something to drink?'

'Sure. There's a bar behind the stage. I'll have a gin and coke.'

Furnival made his way gingerly towards the group. Behind the dais a door led into a smaller room with a bar. He bought the drinks from a dark-skinned young man wearing what looked like a very old llama around his shoulders, and started to thread his way back to his companion. He half expected to find her gone, but she still sat at his table her clown's face gazing towards the musicians.

Furnival put their glasses down.

'Up from the country, are you?' the girl asked kindly.

'That's right, seeing the sights for a few

days. My nephew was coming with me but a friend of his was killed last night, and he didn't feel up to it.'

The girl laughed shortly. 'You don't mean Barbara Jayne, do you?'

'Yes, that was her name. Did you know her?'

'I knew her a bit. She was a real drag. It's a laugh all the boys being so upset when she's dead. Nobody took much notice of her when she was alive. Who's your nephew?'

'His name is Nick Harrington. Who else was upset about Barbara?'

'Oh, Rob Redmond. I suppose you might say he was her fellow, they lived together, well, in the same house. Different flats, all quite respectable.'

'Is he here tonight?'

'Yes, at least I saw him earlier. He was stoned out of his mind.' She looked around. 'There he is, over there.'

Furnival followed her nod. Only a few feet from them at an empty table, and strangely isolated in the crowded room, sat a very large young man. He had a big slab of a face, thick brown hair, and huge shoulders. It looked as though the boy from the top floor and Barbara's regular escort at the Birdcage were one and the same person. His face was very pale and he stared straight ahead of him, endlessly turning his glass in his hands.

Furnival looked around and spotted an almost presentable young man eyeing his companion.

He got up. 'There seems to be a young man over there after my place. I think I'll go and talk to Redmond.'

'You'd better wait a bit,' said the girl. 'Dinah is just coming on. He won't want to be distracted now.'

Furnival had started across the distance between the two tables when every light in the place suddenly went out. There was absolute silence in the darkness. Then very slowly one light grew in the centre of the stage and Dinah Merriman drifted into it. She wore a short golden dress like beaten metal, and golden sandals laced to the knee. Then the music crashed out and she started to dance. Everything the primitive music was supposed to be it was while she danced; hypnotic, abandoned, working to a feverish release. She undulated her golden limbs, her eyes closed, her head flung back showing her lovely throat. The music grew louder and faster towards its climax, and she gyrated faster, totally self-absorbed and unconscious of her silent audience. Then the music stopped dead, the lights went out, and when they came on again she was gone.

The young man sitting alone was still staring at the spot where Dinah had danced.

''Oh, death will find me long before I tire of watching you,'' he said thickly to the empty air.

Furnival slipped into the seat beside him. 'Don't tell me people still read Rupert Brooke.'

Rob Redmond turned round and tried to focus on Furnival. His eyes were blue-grey and glazed with misery. 'He described some states rather well,' he said.

'Like love?'

The young man laughed bitterly. 'No, not like love. Like obsession, like being sick and empty when you're not with the object of it.' He had a slight Australian accent.

'She's very lovely.'

'She's rotten. I quarrelled with my girl over her.'

'And your girl was killed?'

Redmond made another attempt to focus on Furnival's face. 'Did you know Barbara?'

'I know friends of hers.'

'I was her only friend.'

'How was she for enemies?'

'Barbara didn't have enemies — she wasn't the type to arouse strong feelings.'

'Somebody killed her.'

'People seem to think it was some old boy she brought home with her. She was so green she was bound to get in with a wrong one sooner or later.' Redmond produced a bottle of whisky from his jacket pocket and poured it lavishly into his glass. 'I don't know much about it, I haven't been home yet, but that's the version that's going around.'

'Why haven't you been home? The police are sure to want to talk to you.'

'I was on my way home last night at about midnight when I heard what had happened. After that I just couldn't face going in.'

'The police are having difficulty tracing her.'

'She came from the north of England, Lancashire or Yorkshire. I remember her saying she spent her holidays in Blackpool when she was a kid, if that's any help.'

'Oh, great! It narrows it down to about ten millions.'

'I don't get it! Why are you asking me all these questions? Are you working with the police?'

'Emphatically not. What was Barbara like, Rob?'

'She was — rather appealing.' His voice thickened. 'You felt you had to protect her.'

'Somebody didn't.'

Redmond grimaced in pain. 'We parted on bad terms. She was jealous of Dinah, of course.' He gazed again through the crowds and the dizzying lights to the spot where the dancer had performed. 'Dinah was everything Barbara could never be.

She had maximum impact. Barbara knew
I was crazy about her, but what could she
expect? I live next door to her — just ten
feet away. I hear her bathing, dressing,
going to bed — ' His voice broke off.

'When did you move into the house
with the girls?'

Redmond recovered himself. 'About six
months ago, only a week or two before
Barbara. We were thrown together like
innocents abroad. Dinah's been there
about a year.'

'I talked to Dinah earlier. She said she
didn't know any clubs that Barbara
patronized. Didn't she ever see her here?'

'Of course she did. She came out and
sat with Barbara and me sometimes. She
denied that Barbara came to the Birdcage
because Mr. Leslie doesn't want any
more scandal at his club, and Dinah is
Mr. Leslie's girl.'

'Why should there be any scandal just
because Barbara came here? She wasn't
killed here.'

Redmond was silent for a moment.
Then he said, 'No,' so quietly that
Furnival scarcely heard him. 'No, she

wasn't killed here. But Mr. Leslie is rather
— sensitive.'

'What do you know about him?

'He's a gangster.' Redmond caught
Furnival's expression of disbelief. 'He's
mixed up in all the rackets in town
— gambling, girls, protection, God knows
what else. He's got an interest in
half-a-dozen clubs like this. He's rotten
and vicious.'

'Is he here?'

'I just saw him come in. He's to the left
of the door. Any minute now he'll come
across and suggest that I've had too much
to drink and ought to go home. Mr. Leslie
is uneasy about having me in his club.'

Furnival looked around surreptitiously.
He picked out Mr. Leslie instantly. He
was a big man, six feet tall and a little
overweight, in his late twenties. His face
was pink and curiously hairless, and there
was only a little soft down on his head as
though his hair was growing in again after
an illness. He was expensively dressed; on
his wrist he wore a heavy gold bracelet.

Behind him another man lurked, a man
with the air of having no existence of his

own, but living and acting at the beck of another. He was short and enormously broad with massive shoulders. He had a huge face with a broken nose and evil little dark eyes.

'Who's the Missing Link?' asked Furnival.

Redmond grinned. 'Funny you should say that. That is a gentleman generally known as the Ape. He assists Mr. Leslie in his business enterprizes. I said that Mr. Leslie will politely imply that I ought to leave. It's the Ape standing behind his shoulder who adds weight to the suggestion.'

Furnival looked again at the two men. Sure enough they had started to bear down on Rob's table, Mr. Leslie smiling greetings around him as he advanced. They were within ten feet of the table when Leslie suddenly changed direction and swerved away. The Ape came to a confused halt, then followed him.

Furnival felt a gentle hand on his shoulder. He looked up, a long way up.

'I wonder what brings you to this place,' said Superintendent Calvert gently.

8

The superintendent was exquisitely dressed; a hint of midnight blue in his suit, discreet ruffles down his shirt. He pulled a chair up to the table and sat down. 'Do you mind if I join you, Rob?'

'I'm going. I feel sick,' announced Redmond. He got up abruptly and blundered through the dancers to the door.

'Now please don't you go, Mr. Furnival,' begged Calvert. 'I shall develop a complex. As soon as I arrive, people depart hastily in all directions!'

Furnival felt very foolish. 'You know Redmond?'

'You'd be surprised who I know.'

'But don't you want to question him?'

'Don't worry. I have someone waiting for him. But how about you, Furnival, I imagine you know a few people by now?'

'I know that Barbara Jayne came here regularly, and the Birdcage is suspected of drug traffic,' said Furnival.

'Suspected?' Calvert raised an eyebrow. 'You know just how much use suspicion is to us, Furnival. I know a good deal about the Birdcage, and Mr. Leslie. I knew him when he was still Lesnevitch. He's had me once for false arrest and it's not going to happen again. Next time I make quite sure. Meanwhile it's convenient to me to turn a blind eye to the Birdcage. I can pick up tips here. I can pick up people here. It's easier than finding new locations all the time.'

'What about the Ape?'

'He's just Leslie's muscle. A brute, an ex-con, he's done stretches for every charge in the book.'

'Is there someone behind Leslie?'

'Of course. Two very fragrant brothers called Blaikie from the East End. And please don't take off after them. If no one blunders in and messes up the operation I may get them put away before so very long.'

'Redmond says that Dinah Merriman is Leslie's girl?'

'Yes, so I believe. I admit I was

interested when I heard that she had a room in the same house as Barbara. She'd do anything to cover up for Leslie.'

Furnival thought of the coloured girl dancing in the spotlight, the golden light dappling her like sunshine.

Calvert caught his expression. 'Don't think too harshly of her. She's using the only thing she has. She's only got about ten years at her best. What else is there for her — hash slinging at a Corner House?'

'Redmond and Barbara were friendly,' said Furnival. 'But they had quarrelled over Dinah. I scarcely found out anything else. Nobody seems to have known Barbara well.'

'No, we still haven't traced her beyond her previous digs. Barbara Jayne is obviously a phoney; possibly her Christian names.'

'Doesn't Gino have her insurance card?'

'He says he never had it. Oh, we'll trace her all right, but it may take a little time. Dozens of these girls go missing every week, usually from the North, attracted to the bright lights of swinging London.'

Calvert grimaced bitterly remembering Barbara Jayne's lifeless body beneath the brilliant mortuary lights.

'She had too much money,' said Furnival.

'I know. Most girls share flats in London, but she was paying out eight guineas a week. Gino wouldn't be paying her very much.'

'He said he wasn't — he implied she wasn't worth a full salary. What is Gino's background?'

'He's all right. Four years in Linden Terrace, eight years before that in a more modest place in Evers Street. No breath of trouble against him.'

'But you will admit that there's a link between Barbara and this crowd.' Furnival had lowered his voice. The live group had given place to a record player, and it was possible to hear normal conversation. 'I know there was no one except Mrs. Marshall and Mrs. Cobbett in that house when Gerald was discovered with the body, but someone could have left immediately after killing Barbara. Mrs. Cobbett wasn't on watch just at that time.

I think that Marian Smith, like Gerald, is just an innocent who blundered into a mess. There may be all sorts of reasons why she is lying low. Redmond, too, strikes me as quite innocent. But Dinah Merriman is in up to her neck with some very nasty characters.'

'I'm afraid I'm not prepared to write Harrington off yet,' said Calvert. 'The type of murder he would have committed is still more common than a gang killing. They're business men, they don't kill if they can avoid it. And don't write young Redmond off either.' He broke off and absently patted the rump of a passing young girl who had draped her arms around his neck. 'Not now, Cindy, Uncle is busy!' He turned back to Furnival. 'I've had my eye on him for a long time.'

'On Redmond? What for?'

'About six months ago a young man was killed here in my manor. He was a junkie, and he was found beaten to death in an alley.'

'David Summers,' murmured Furnival.

'Oh, you've heard about him? Well, Rob Redmond and David Summers were very close friends. In fact they shared a flat together. After Summers died, Redmond moved into Avery Street where he befriended Barbara. When death follows someone around so closely, I keep my eye on them.'

'Wasn't there another girl, too?'

'You mean Linda Todd? Linda's death was suicide, I'm positive of that. Doubt was only raised because she was Summer's girl, and because she was an addict. It's no use your interfering here, Furnival. There are connections and complications it would take you years to fathom.'

Furnival looked around him at the outlandishly dressed youngsters, spoilt, avid for kicks, as ripe for ignition as dry tinder.

'I don't envy you,' he said. 'Do you really think Redmond is involved?'

'I think he knows something useful he could tell me. I'm almost sure Summers got his dope from the Birdcage. For the last six weeks of his life he scarcely went anywhere else. Redmond swears he has no idea where he got the stuff. Summers was at the L.S.E. before he dropped out.

He was a particularly attractive young man, with a great gift for making friends, and he was intelligent before he was destroyed. Yet Redmond is still hanging around this place, even after they got his girl hooked too. Why? Because it's the gay, groovy place where everyone goes? Well, perhaps, if he forgives easily.'

Furnival thought of the misery and rage in Redmond's eyes. 'I don't think he forgives easily,' he said. 'Is he on dope himself?'

'He wasn't. And I don't think anyone would start who had watched Summers go down the drain. No, it's my idea that Redmond is brewing up some personal revenge of his own for Leslie.'

'Would that matter?'

'Yes, it would. I don't want to pick up a couple of tuppenny-ha-penny pushers, I'm quite aware that pills change hands here, and hash is smoked. I've got a nose. I want to know where the bulk of the heroin is coming from, and that's going to take more patience and discretion than Redmond has. You know, it's quite a problem for me keeping Mr. Leslie alive, there must be so many parents and friends and lovers who have seen their loved ones destroyed, just itching to get at him.'

'So there is nothing I can do, unofficially?'

'No, thanks. And there's another thing, call Landseer off. I don't want him hanging around.'

'What's the matter with him? He's an ex-copper, isn't he?'

'An ex-copper, yes. Not a retired copper. He was dismissed.'

'What for?'

'A lot of things. Landseer was good at one time, there was no one better at bringing in information. He had marvellous contacts, but like others before him with a lot of contact in the criminal world he started to identify with them. He was doing too many deals, too many people had to be paid off in favours, and too many perks were slipping his way.'

'Don't you ever use him?'

'I wouldn't let him within a mile of a case of mine. He's scruffy, he boozes, and he's a disgrace to the Force. So keep him out of my hair.' Calvert looked genuinely furious. 'I'm off now,' he said suddenly. 'I can't waste any more time here.'

'Wait!' said Furnival. 'You will check their alibis, won't you? Leslie, the Ape, Dinah — all that bunch.'

'Don't worry, Furnival, I shall leave no stone unturned! But in the case of Leslie and the Ape personal alibis aren't worth much. They're professionals, they commission killings.'

Furnival watched him as he threaded his way through the crowd, apart from them, yet, like all good detectives, quite accepted by them. He sat on alone for a few minutes. The music by now had a hypnotic effect and he began to feel sleepy. He thought how amazingly the day was ending after its beginning in his semi in the quiet Meddenham suburb. He should have been painting the kitchen tonight, and here he was — making the scene.

He looked around him. Some of the young people were pale and glassy-eyed probably from lack of sleep and fresh air. On the whole they didn't look happy, but he saw no suspicious little packets change hands, and no one approached him with an offer to pour out their hearts. He decided to leave. Outside it was very cold. Although it was only eleven o'clock the street was as quiet as Meddenham. No painted ladies beckoned to him from doorways, no fiendish orientals slunk down alleys. He saw only two marauding cats and a distant policeman before he located his car.

He turned back to Joliphant Gardens, parked the car in the forecourt and climbed the stairs to the Harringtons' flat. Gerald and Nicky were in the living-room waiting for him. Gerald had a large whisky in his hand and looked as though it was the last of several. From the smaller bedroom Furnival could hear Elaine and Joanna making up beds.

Gerald rose rather unsteadily and clasped his hand. 'Glad you're back, old man,' he said thickly. 'Been the longest day of my life.'

'Has anything happened?'

Gerald glanced cautiously towards the bedroom door. 'Marian telephoned,' he whispered. Furnival sat down. 'What did she say?'

'It was exactly what I thought might have happened. She was held up at her hairdressers. It's only a few doors from the house, and she was there when it was all going on. Word blew into the shop, and the customers saw the whole thing, Barbara being taken away in an ambulance, me being taken in a police car, everything.'

'Do you mean to say she just lurked there watching?' broke in Nicky indignantly. 'Didn't she rush out and attempt to wrench you from the police?'

'Shut up, Nicky,' said Furnival, although something similar had crossed his mind. 'What does she intend to do, Gerald? Is she going to the police?'

'She's thinking about it.'

'*Thinking about it?* But, good God, she must come forward! She's the only thing to tie you to the house.'

'Put yourself in her shoes, Matthew,' said Gerald miserably. 'Her parents are very old, and ultra-respectable, the shock could kill them. She's promised to speak out if it becomes really essential.'

'Like when you're standing on the trap door?' enquired Nicky sweetly.

Furnival studied his brother-in-law covertly. He really knew very little about him. The beefy face and small blue eyes, always a little glazed by overmuch social drinking, had only suggested stupidity to him. Could there be brutality, too? Had he allowed the colourful, dramatic ambience of the Birdcage to beguile him from the more likely solution? Calvert was used to this background and he still thought that Gerald was very much in the running. But now, after Marian's phone call, surely Gerald could be eliminated? If he was expecting her to return to the flat at any moment he was unlikely to have murdered Barbara while he waited.

He realized that Joanna and Elaine had come in from the bedroom and were regarding him anxiously.

'Did you go to that club, Matthew?' asked Joanna.

'The Birdcage? Yes, I've been there all evening. Do you know it, Nicky?'

'I've been there once or twice.'

'Did you ever see Barbara there?'

'No, I never saw her anywhere except Gino's.'

'Do you know a Rob Redmond who used to escort her? A big Australian, about twenty years old? No? Well, what about Dinah Merriman, the dancer?'

'Did I know her? No, I regret to say. I've seen her — she's terrific — but that's all. She keeps herself to herself.'

'And to Mr. Leslie?'

'So they say.'

'She lived in the house where Barbara was killed.'

Nicky was surprised. 'I didn't know that. I should have thought Leslie would have set her up in better style than Avery Street.'

'What's the matter with Avery Street?' Gerald was drunkenly stung in defence of his love nest. 'Christ! it was setting me back ten quid a week.'

'What?' yelped Elaine. 'It's a damned sight too good for whores, I should say.'

'Keep your cool, for God's sake,' begged Nicky. 'What I meant was, Mr.Leslie's supposed to be loaded.'

'Did you ever hear of drugs changing hands at the Birdcage?' asked Furnival.

Nicky hesitated. 'Well, I know pillheads go there,' he said. 'I suppose there's no harm in telling you that, they go everywhere. I can't tell you any names anyway, because I don't know any.'

'What do they take? Amphetamines?'

'Yes, they take Bennies and Black Bombers and French Blues. They cost about two bob each. They take them to stay awake.'

'What about cannabis?' pressed Furnival.

'Yes, a few smoke pot, the coloured mostly. But, like the pills, it just changes hands among the kids. I've never heard that the management was involved.'

'What about hard drugs? Heroin for instance?'

'I've never heard any rumours of that.'

'What are you going to do next?' asked Joanna.

'I don't think I should do anything — no listen, Elaine — I'm sure there will be very little trouble extricating Gerald. His friend has assured him she'll come forward and tell the police why he was in the room at that time. This case is probably part of a much larger set-up a gang of professional criminals, of which I'm completely ignorant. I could mess the whole thing up for the police.'

There was a silence. 'I think Matthew is right,' said Joanna surprisingly. 'A big element in police work is being familiar with the local background and people.'

'So what do you want to do?' asked Nicky. 'Go home?'

'I'll certainly stay on here until it's over, if it's any comfort to you. Calvert doesn't seem to object to talking things over with me, and I'll admit I'm interested. What I'm going to do right now is go to bed, and I think the first thing to be done tomorrow is to call off Landseer.'

9

Furnival set off before nine the following morning for Landseer's address. He found the house without difficulty, it was another of the terraced type he was getting so familiar with, the shabbiest yet. It was in a decaying neighbourhood; doors and railings were unpainted, dingy curtains covered the windows, and ancient prams stood at many of the steps. Furnival pushed open the squeaking area gate and descended the worn steps where ferns sprouted dankly. He pounded on the basement door, but there was no answer. He knocked again; perhaps the veteran sleuth was still sleeping, he had not impressed Furnival as an early riser. He looked up at a noise behind him. The faces of three small boys, one black, one blonde, and one pale chocolate, peered through the gate at him.

'Have you seen Mr. Landseer go out this morning?' he called up to them.

There was a conference between the children. 'No, he ain't gone out, Mister.' The black boy, elected spokesman, flashed a grin. 'P'raps he's drunk, he had a party last night. Cor, you should 'ave heard the noise!'

Furnival felt suddenly cold. 'What kind of noise?' he asked. 'Was it music? Singing?'

'No, not music. It was sort of thumping and crashing about. I know 'cos I sleeps in the room above.'

Furnival turned back, tried the handle, and was surprised to find the door open. He slipped inside and closed it on the curious children. Inside the basement room was very dark, but even in the gloom he could see evidence of violent commotion. He stepped over a smashed chair to the window, and pulled back the curtains. A scene of complete and mindless chaos met his eyes. All the smaller pieces of furniture in the room had been smashed, pictures and vases had been torn down and shattered. Broken fragments of crockery, beer and whisky bottles crunched underfoot.

He heard a faint noise from the room beyond, a rasping, indrawn breath, dead silence as the breath was held, then Landseer's voice, weak and rough with fear.

'Who — who is it?'

Furnival moved to the back room. Here, too, the vandals had smashed and ripped, but Furnival's eyes went immediately to the bed and to Landseer. He lay on the bed in a pair of striped pyjamas and an old knitted cardigan. His face was swollen and bruised, and his eyes were so puffy around as to be almost invisible. An inch long slit bisected his upper lip, and there was a lump the size of a walnut at his hairline. The front of his pyjamas was daubed in blood.

Furnival hurried to the bed and knelt beside the older man. 'I'll call a doctor,' he said. 'You'd better get into hospital.'

Landseer stopped him with a gesture. 'No,' he said, and winced at the pain of moving his gashed mouth. 'No — nothing broken. I've been done over before, I know the signs. Whisky in the bottom drawer, I think they left one intact, the bastards.'

Furnival hurried to get a basin of water

and some cloths, and began to gently bathe Landseer's face. 'Who did this?' he asked in quiet rage.

'He was waiting for me when I got back last night. About eleven o'clock.'

'The Ape?'

'I think so.'

'Was he alone?'

'With the Ape it only takes one.'

Furnival finished sponging Landseer's face, found a clean pyjama jacket in a drawer, helped him into it, and pulled the blankets over him. He poured a large whisky, and put it into Landseer's ready hand.

'We ought to let the police know,' he said.

'Calvert? Christ, no, I'd sooner face the Ape again.'

Furnival sat on the end of the bed and lit cigarettes for both of them. 'What do you think set them off? What had you been up to?'

'I was at the Birdcage, the club I told you about.'

'I was there for a couple of hours. I didn't see you.'

'I was upstairs chatting up the staff. There are usually three or four young blokes hanging about, barmen, bouncers, that kind of thing, and the band, of course.'

'The group? The Zebra Zodiacs? What do you make of them?'

'I don't think they know anything. They live for their music!' Landseer winced as the liquor touched his damaged lip.

'What did you ask them?'

'I asked them if they had known Barbara Jayne, if they ever saw her upstairs in Mr. Leslie's flat, and if anybody at the Birdcage seemed particularly close to her.'

'Brother, you asked for it! What's this about Leslie's flat? Surely he doesn't live there?'

'He just has a bed in his office, and a little bathroom fixed up next door. He sleeps there occasionally when he's very late. He's got a beautiful house out at Richmond.'

'You seem to know a lot about it.'

'Oh, well — I've been around a long time.'

'What did they say?'

'They all denied any knowledge of Barbara.'

'Did you speak to Dinah Merriman?'

'No, I didn't see her, or Leslie or the Ape, but obviously someone told them I'd been around. I just spoke to three young blokes I know have worked there for some time, and the boys in the band. Oh, one of the young chaps did ask me if I was working for Gino.'

'For Gino?'

'Yes, he said he knew Gino was 'just dying to get something on the boss'.'

'Gino did tell me that Barbara went to clubs he didn't think very suitable, but he didn't specifically mention the Birdcage.'

Furnival stood up. 'It seems feeble to say I'm sorry about this, Landseer. I was just about to call you off. Harrington or I will send you a cheque for your services and the damage to your place.'

Landseer gestured helplessly. 'My services? I don't reckon they were worth much. I couldn't do anything to help your brother-in-law.'

'I'm not sure about that. Surely the fact

that Leslie had you roughed up proves
that he has something to hide.'

'Furnival, Mr. Leslie has a thousand
things to hide, and they could be sweet
damn-all to do with Barbara Jayne.'

'You could be right. Well I'll do my best
to get it about that you've lost all interest
in the case. Do you think you'll be safe
here?'

'Oh, yes. They know I scare easily.'

'Well, keep your door locked.'

Furnival walked out to the area. The
little coloured boy was now alone, sitting
on the steps.

'Do you know Mr. Landseer, lad?'
Furnival asked.

'Yes, sir, he's a friend of mine.'

Furnival put two half crowns into the
boy's hand. 'He's had an accident. Will
you look in on him a couple of times, see
if he's all right, and if he needs anything?
And if you hear any more thumping and
crashing from his room beat it like hell for
a grown-up.'

He got into his car and drove to Avery
Street deep in thought. He was convinced
that the action of Leslie and his

henchmen in beating up Landseer was an admission of guilt, if not of Barbara's death, at least of her drug addiction. But how to get at them? Drugs of every description could change hands in their club and they could plead innocence of what was going on quite convincingly. All sorts of things could happen in that crowded, noisy, dimly lit room without them seeing a thing. What he needed was a decoy looking for heroin, but he was aware of his limitations as an actor, and the role was too risky to entrust to anyone else.

When he got to Avery Street two or three curious spectators were hanging around the house. He pushed past them and climbed the steps. The doors to the vestibule stood open, and he decided to go up to Redmond's room unannounced. There was no sign of life on the first floor and the police seals were still intact; Furnival continued noiselessly up the uncarpeted flight to the second floor. He knocked at the door he took to be Redmond's and after a few moments a thick voice bade him come in. Furnival entered. Redmond, like Landseer, was sprawled on the bed, but his face was unmarked by anything beyond the previous evening's excesses. The room was chaotically untidy, books and papers, all covered with a film of dust, lay piled on every surface, together with unwashed dishes and discarded clothes. The room had the air of a life marking time.

The young man on the bed pushed his tousled hair off his face and peered at Furnival through bleary eyes.

'What the hell — ?' he began.

'I'm sorry to disturb you.' Furnival sat down calmly on a relatively unlittered chair. 'I wanted to talk some more.'

Redmond turned on his side, humped the blankets over his head and muttered an unmistakeable invitation to Furnival to leave.

Furnival looked around, found a sponge bag and towel, dragged aside the bedclothes, and dropped them on Redmond's face.

'Get up!' he said. 'I'm not playing games. I believe you wanted to nail Leslie once, until his girl sidetracked you. I want him stopped before he cuts a swathe through all the neurotic kids in this district.'

Redmond sat up and rested his head on his knees. 'I don't know a thing,' he said.

'Then it won't take long to tell me about it. You said last night that Leslie didn't like you hanging around the club. Why not?'

'I don't know. Perhaps he doesn't think I'm much of an advertisement for swinging London.' Redmond climbed out of bed and peered in the dressing table mirror. 'Look at me, he could be right. I sit there in the merry throng looking like Banquo's ghost — the spectre at the feast. I went there with David, he died. I went there with Linda, and she died. I went there with Barbara, now she is dead. I'm a jinx.'

'Yes, you are, aren't you?' agreed Furnival. 'You lived in the same house as Summers, too, didn't you? And then here with Barbara? And Dinah Merriman, who is closely linked to Leslie and the Birdcage, lives here also. All coincidence?'

The young man rummaged through a

pile of clothes, selected the least grubby sweater and pulled it on.

'Not the last,' he said. 'Not Dinah living here — that wasn't a coincidence.' He sat down on the bed. 'Look, I don't know who the hell you are, mister, but I know you're in with the police — you were with Calvert last night. So I'll tell you everything I know, and then you can leave me alone.

'David and I roomed together for more than a year. He was intelligent, but a bit highly strung. He came from somewhere in Surrey. His father was in business in a small town, a big cheese in the town, or so he liked to think. He reckoned everyone in the town watched everything his family did. David came to London for anonymity, and before he died he was as anonymous as a bit of dirt on the street. He had been taking pep pills for a long time, and I think he had just started on heroin when I moved in with him. After about three months he gave up even trying to go to school anymore. His whole life became one long hustle for dope. He was treated by two different doctors, first a private one who dumped him when he was unable to pay, and then a National Health man who dumped him for stealing prescriptions. He tried a cure three times but he couldn't take it.

'In the early days David went out a lot,' went on Redmond. 'But in the last three months he hardly went anywhere except the Birdcage. The same with Linda, his girlfriend, she went there a lot. And other junkies I've known — they haven't died, they're taking treatment, or they've just drifted away — but more patrons of the Birdcage than similar clubs seem to get on to dope.'

'But David never told you he obtained it there?' put in Furnival.

'He would never tell me where he got it. But when he died I felt I had to dig up something. The police didn't seem to be doing anything. I didn't know where to begin. I'd never seen drugs change hands. I'd never seen David speak to Mr Leslie. I couldn't get near Leslie where he lived, at Richmond. All I could do was hang around the club. Then I heard there was a room vacant in this house where his girl lived. I thought that might be an opening, Dinah spends a lot of time with him, so I took it.'

'And Barbara?'

'Barbara just turned up here a couple of weeks after me. I didn't know her from Adam, but we got friendly. She was a sweet kid, and I needed someone to take to the Birdcage; I though it would look more natural. I suppose I was responsible for introducing her to the place. Nothing happened to harm her while she was with me, but in the last few weeks she had taken to going on her own.'

'Did you learn anything from Dinah?'

'Not a thing. She was very sweet to me, but she would never talk about Leslie or the Birdcage. She has a lot of people up in her flat, but he never came here.'

Redmond got off the bed and drifted into the kitchen. He rinsed two cups under the tap and spooned coffee powder into them. His voice came rather muffled back to Furnival.

'And then, as you say, I was side-tracked. I was so besotted with Dinah that I was afraid to do, or think, anything for fear it linked her to that scum.'

'You know she's linked to them!'

Redmond gave his whole attention to filling the two cups with boiling water. He carried them carefully out to the living-room, then returned for a bottle of milk and a sugar bowl.

'I'll swear she knows very little of what goes on,' he said. 'Coloureds don't have anything to do with heroin. A lot of them smoke pot, but I've never heard of one on hard drugs.'

'I never suggested she was on them herself.' Furnival took a drink of his coffee. 'Tell me about the night Summers was killed. He *was* killed, wasn't he?'

'He was dying anyway.'

'He was beaten to death. He was your friend, you can't be so obsessed by this woman to have forgotten that. Tell me about the last night he was alive.'

'He was very ill, almost too weak to dress himself, it was horrible to see. I knew he was out of dope. He'd been on the phone almost continually for a week, pleading with all his contacts trying to hustle some, but he couldn't score anywhere. He hadn't got much money, and I think they'd got the wind up; they knew he was dying, and a death means a lot of trouble for everyone until it blows over.

'I had to go out myself that night,' continued Redmond. 'I hated to leave David alone, but I'd been given tickets to a concert and I'd promised to take a girl. In any case, you couldn't 'keep him company'. He was all alone, no one could get near him by then. All I could do was try to keep him safe, and irritate him as little as possible. Then, just before I had to leave, he said he was going out. I pleaded with him not to. He was so weak, and it was a very cold night, but I couldn't change his mind. He said he was only going along to the Birdcage for an hour. When I left the flat at seven o'clock he was still there but he was ready to leave. When I got in at eleven the police were waiting for me. David had been picked up dead in an alley an hour earlier.'

'And he actually said he was going to the Birdcage?' asked Furnival.

'Yes, he did. But no one saw him there that night, and the alley where he was found wasn't directly on his route from the club to our flat. There was nothing to connect him with the place.'

'I bet there wasn't. How exactly was he killed? I mean what was he beaten with?'

'With fists, just with fists. It wouldn't have taken much.'

'Did you ever think of posing as an addict and asking around at the Birdcage for drugs?'

'I tried it a couple of times. No one ever swallowed the bait. I think they were suspicious of me because I'd railed against the place when David died.'

'Did you know Barbara was on drugs?'

'No, I honestly didn't know. I knew she took a lot of pills, but nothing else. If I had known I'd have stopped her some-how.'

'Did she ever mention previous boy-friends?'

'No, she never mentioned the past at all. She thought all her life was in the future.'

Furnival stood up to go. 'Thank you for

talking to me, Rob. I am with the police, but I'm not officially on this case, I'm what is called 'an interested party'. I suggest you continue to keep your eyes and ears open, tell Superintendent Calvert anything you hear, and be careful!'

He went slowly down the stairs to the street. If it were true it was a vile crime, a spider's web baited with music and gaiety for the young and lonely. If he had Calvert's job how he would pursue these fiends — like an avenging angel!

But he had not Calvert's job, and he had no doubt that the other man was better qualified for it. It was right that he should withdraw, and he determined to spend the afternoon as a tourist. A visit to the National Gallery seemed a pleasant prospect, with a mildly extravagant lunch somewhere first. And Elaine should accompany them if she felt inclined — it would take her mind off her worries.

When he reached the Harringtons' apartment Elaine and Joanna were alone in the living-room. They looked pale and frightened.

'What's the matter?' said Furnival immediately.

'There was a phone call,' said Joanna. 'Just a minute ago. They asked for you, by name. Elaine said you were out, but I was here, so they said I was to give you a message.'

'Who are 'they'?'

'It was a man, he wouldn't say who he was. He had a soft voice, a sort of refined cockney. I can't tell you how unpleasant it was! He said he didn't know whose private snoop you were, but to lay off, or he'd have you worked over like Landseer!'

10

'What do you want to do?' asked Furnival. 'Do you want to go home?'

Joanna glanced at her sister. 'It would be the best way of convincing them you weren't going to interfere anymore,' she said.

Furnival had sketched in the situation, as far as he knew it for the women, beginning with who Landseer was, and what had befallen him.

'But who *are* they?' echoed Elaine.

'They're a gang, an organized gang. They have a finger in a lot of rackets, including, I think, pushing drugs to kids. Their front man runs this club, the Birdcage. I believe it's the drug outlet, but I can't see any way to prove it.'

Joanna shivered. 'Oh, Matthew, I do wish we were back among our own homely villains!'

'I think it would be better if you went home,' said Elaine. 'Calvert seems to have lost interest in Gerald. As it is you've drawn this gang's attention to us. Nicky could be in danger!'

'All right,' said Furnival. 'But we'll stay until tomorrow morning Elaine, if that's O.K. with you. I refuse to be in London without one afternoon's innocent enjoyment.' He put his projected plan to the women, but they vetoed it saying that they would feel safer in the flat. Furnival decided to skip the lunch, not feeling his mood would benefit from the extravagance, and, after a snack in the kitchen, departed alone.

He took the tube to St James Park, where he passed an hour before turning down The Mall for Trafalgar Square and the National Gallery. He spent a happy two hours in the Gallery. So absorbed was he that he had visited half-a-dozen galleries before he became aware that he had a companion. Wherever he happened to go, the slight, olive-skinned young man in the lavender coloured suit was ever with him, always keeping to the other end of the room, and most certainly not looking at pictures.

Furnival tried a few tricks, returning to galleries they had already thoroughly 'done', spending an extravagant amount of time before one picture, speeding through whole rooms without stopping for a glance. His companion stuck like pigment. Although not crowded, there were too many people around for there to be any danger of a knife between the shoulder blades, and Furnival began to enjoy himself, lingering maddeningly over old favourites, until the young man's initial expression of bright interest had faded, and his fashionable shoes were plainly killing him.

It was after five o'clock before Furnival slowly descended the steps of the Gallery into Trafalgar Square. He circled the fountains for a few minutes cooing at the pigeons while his shadow sank exhausted on to a bench. Then he set off down the Strand at a brisk pace, thankful that early years of leg work stood him in good stead. He came to a coffee bar, where he perched at the counter and ordered coffee. As he was being served Lavender Suit tottered in and took the table near the door.

Furnival toyed with the idea of taking him to a lengthy session at the British Museum, but decided instead to make the poor fellow's day by paying a visit to Gino's. He was leaving the tube station, only a hundred yards from Gino's shop, before it struck him that his action may have placed the hairdresser in some danger.

Inside the salon, Gino and Terry were still working on the last two customers. Gino glanced over at him with expressionless eyes. John was fussing about accompanied by a menial tidying up. When he saw Furnival he flounced up with a squeal of delight.

'Why, it's Nicky's uncle back again. How marvellous! But I mustn't say uncle, must I? What an image! Now, are you going to let me create something fabulous for you?'

'No, no!' said Furnival hastily, realizing that he was being led to the centre of operations. He thought of his superintendent's face confronted with 'super Sable Highlights'. 'I'm sorry, but in the Force

we are expected to have more or less
regulation haircuts.'

'Oh, poor you, how absolutely awful. I
should just leave!' John pouted wistfully.
'I could have done something gorgeous
for you, too, you've got such a lovely lot
of hair. I could bring out those
marvellous tawny highlights, and shape it
to take off some of that rugged look. Your
jaw is much too square.'

'I'm sorry — ' began Furnival.

'Well, it's just that it's not *in* now. Your
type had a good run, you know. Now,
Superintendent Calvert I could do
wonders with — such a theatrical man!'

'I only came to say goodbye,' Furnival
broke in firmly. 'I'm leaving tomorrow.'
He drew John into a cubicle away from
the other men.

'I wanted to talk about a place called
the Birdcage,' he murmured.

'The club in Alder Court?'

'You know it?'

'I've been there a couple of times.'

'Do you know Mr Leslie?'

'Of course I do. We used to do his hair
up until a couple of months ago.'

'What happened then?'

'Gino had a row with him. He told him he didn't want him to come here anymore.'

'That sounds rather courageous of Gino — or foolhardy.'

'Stupid I should call it. He lost a lot of business. It wasn't only Mr Leslie — his friends and staff, and the entertainers from the club all used to come in.'

'The Ape, too?'

John giggled. 'Come off it! There are limits to my talent. Anyway, I thought it was a shame when they stopped coming. They were fun, and they were good tippers, too.'

'So Barbara would have seen Leslie here in the salon? Did she have much to do with him?'

'No. Just to say hello. She didn't manicure him.'

'I wonder why Gino quarrelled with him?'

'I wouldn't know, dear. Gino kept it very discreet. But it could have been over Barbara going to the Birdcage. Gino was terribly stuffy over her.'

'He told me she went to clubs he didn't approve of,' said Furnival. 'But he said he had no idea where she got her drugs.'

'She was on drugs?' John's eyes widened. 'Oh, the silly girl. I've tried pot, it made me dreadfully sick, but not hard drugs. They're *death* to the looks.'

'They're death,' said Furnival.

'Well, I suppose she might have got them from the Birdcage, but I don't know why Gino kicked up a fuss all of a sudden. Everybody knows you can get any commodity from Mr. Leslie.'

Gino bowed his customer out, and joined them in the cubicle. 'More questions, Mr. Furnival?'

'Matthew is leaving town tomorrow,' put in John. 'He just came to say goodbye.'

'I'm glad to hear it. No offence, Mr. Furnival, but I think all this business is better left to the man on the job.'

'I agree,' said Furnival heartily. 'I was a complete innocent hitting out in the dark. The Metropolitan Police know all about the heroin angle, and the Birdcage, and Mr. Leslie and his friends.'

Gino's tanned skin turned a sickly ivory. John looked uneasily from one man to the other, like a child whose party turns out to be not much fun.

'Did you finish clearing up, John?' Gino asked him.

'Not quite. Not where you were working.'

'Get on with it, would you? Come into the back,' he invited Furnival.

Furnival followed Gino once more down the passage to the homely little room behind the shop. Again Gino slumped into his swivel chair.

'You didn't tell me about the Birdcage, Gino,' said Furnival.

'I didn't want you to get into any trouble. A man can get hurt tangling with Mr Leslie.'

'John tells me you refused his custom.'

'It was just a gesture, it was all I could do.' Gino lit a cigarette rather shakily. 'I'm no hero, but I knew David Summers. I was fond of him, he was a fine young man. He deserved a better life than he had — and more of it.'

'Do you know how he died?'

'They killed him. No, I know nothing of his end. They killed him the day he took his first shot of heroin. I lied to you, Mr Furnival, I'm not quite ignorant of drugs, I've seen several young men who used to come to my shop, who took a great pride in their appearance, dragged down by their use. People think drugs are taken by the bold swinging set, the trendsetters, but they're not. They're taken by people who need an extra little bit of insulation.

'About David, he was always trying to hustle drugs at the end, he thought of nothing else. He would even hang around here pestering my customers. I met him the week before he died, he was very weak and rambling, almost incoherent. He kept saying he'd got to get to the Birdcage.'

'Did he say why? To get his supply?'

'No, he didn't.'

'And you've never heard of drug trafficking on a large scale? I'm thinking of something quite different from what we have had in England — addicts selling part of their prescriptions to one another. I'm thinking of something more on the

American style, large quantities smuggled in from abroad in the way cannabis is. Calvert thinks it could never happen when addicts can get their requirements legally from a doctor, but I'm not sure. The number of heroin addicts is rocketing, and registered addicts swear they never sell their prescriptions to non-users, only to other addicts in need. These new customers are getting it from somewhere.'

'A market could be built up,' said Gino. 'I've heard of plenty of junkies who would sooner die than register with a doctor. A doctor is legally bound to attempt a cure, and, in the case of a minor, contact his parents. Anyway, doctors who would touch drug cases were always harder to find than you'd imagine, and those who did get registered with one never considered they were given enough. And now with the new legislation setting up treatment centres, and their own doctors not allowed to prescribe for them anymore, the addicts will be getting even more alarmed.'

Gino reached into the bottom drawer

of his desk and took out a bottle of sherry and two glasses. He filled the glasses and passed one across the desk to Furnival.

'We keep it for medicinal purposes. Sometimes when one of the boys' wilder creations hasn't turned out just as they dreamed it up they can get in quite a state!

'I never heard of any traffic in drugs,' he went on. 'But if it exists the Birdcage would be an ideal place. Crowds of kids with money to spend and eager for kicks. No adult supervision. The groups moving about the country all the time.'

'And when you have a real drug underworld you get all the attendant crime that moves in with it,' said Furnival. 'Most addicts soon become incapable of doing a job, they have to steal and prostitute to raise the price of a fix, and there are further pickings for a ruthless operator who can exploit that angle.' He looked around the little back room as he drank his sherry, trying to imagine Barbara Jayne pouring out her heart here to Gino. It seemed an unlikely relationship.

'John said you were leaving,' said Gino.

'Yes, I'm going tomorrow. I never had any right to be here anyway.'

'Did you find out anything?'

'No,' said Furnival. He put down his sherry glass and got up to go. 'Not a thing.'

He went back to the salon unescorted, let himself out into the area, and mounted the steps to the street. It was almost dusk and Furnival's eyes were still accustomed to the brightly lit room. He did not see the patient figure in the lavender-coloured suit detach itself from a nearby doorway and drift after him.

It was eight o'clock when he arrived back at the Harrington flat, and he was pleased to find Joanna alone, curled up on the divan looking absurdly attractive.

He put his lips to her ear. 'Alone at last.'

'Don't be silly,' said Joanna, but she swung her feet down to make room beside her. 'Elaine is in the kitchen. Did you have a good day?'

'Very pleasant.' Furnival decided not to worry her with Lavender Suit. 'Anything happen here while I was out?'

'Not a thing, it's almost an anti-climax. Are we really going tomorrow?'

Furnival moved closer and rested his head in the crook of his wife's shoulder. 'We are really going.'

Elaine burst in from the kitchen. 'Oh, there you are at last, Matthew.' She looked at them. 'Not necking after ten years of marriage — good God, it's obscene.'

'Nice, though,' murmured Furnival.

Elaine set him a place at the table, and the three of them discussed the events of the last few days while he ate his supper. It was nearly nine o'clock when the telephone rang. Elaine answered it somewhat nervously.

'It's for you,' she said to Furnival. 'It's Superintendent Calvert.'

Furnival took the receiver, rather surprised to be hearing from Calvert again.

'Ah, Furnival, still with us then?' Calvert's voice came over the wire so urbane that Furnival could see the lifted eyebrow.

'I'm leaving tomorrow.'

'I hope I haven't chased you away. Actually I wanted a word with you. I have someone here with me you may be interested in meeting. Miss Marian Smith. Why don't you come over?'

Furnival hastily finished his coffee, said goodbye to the women, and went down to his car.

Calvert was lounging back in his chair. At a desk against the wall, the plump balding detective Furnival had noticed on his previous visit was seated. In front of Calvert's desk sat a neat dark-haired young woman in the sort of pastel dress and jacket that Furnival associated with white gloves and weddings.

'Miss Smith,' smiled Calvert. 'I'd like you to meet Detective-Inspector Furnival. He is Gerald Harrington's brother-in-law.'

The girl turned quickly in her chair. She was not very young, probably almost thirty, and not exceptionally pretty. She smiled up at Furnival looking near to tears, and tentatively extended her hand.

'How do you do, Mr Furnival? Oh,

whatever must Gerry think of me, not
coming forward before? But I didn't see I
could be any help to him.' She had a
genteel South London accent.

'I expect you were upset and confused,
Miss Smith,' said Furnival kindly.
'Anyway, you're here now.'

'Of course she doesn't alibi him,' said
Calvert. 'But she does give him a reason
for being in the room at that time. Now
all we need is a reason for Barbara being
there.'

'I can't help you there,' said Marian
Smith. 'I wasn't friendly with the girl.'

'Did you ever talk to her?' asked
Furnival.

'Not if I could help it. She used to try
to waylay me on the stairs to chat, but I
brushed her off. We didn't have anything
in common.'

'She never confided anything to you?'

'Good gracious, no!'

'I've been talking to Miss Smith for an
hour,' interrupted Calvert. 'She can't tell
us anything except that she has a
cast-iron alibi.'

'I can vouch for Gerry's character,' said

Marian Smith. 'He would never have done anything like that. Even when he was — er — emotionally roused he was always a perfect gentleman. Please, Mr. Calvert, can't you keep us out of it? If our relationship comes out it would look so bad, as if he had set me up in an apartment like a common — '

'Prostitute?' suggested Calvert sweetly.

'Well, yes. I'm sure a girl like that must have had a lot of unsavoury acquaintances, it was just unfortunate that I happened to live there.'

'I'll see what I can do,' said Calvert. 'I have your address, Miss Smith. I'll contact you again if I need to.' He saw the girl out and returned to his desk. He turned to Furnival.

'Pretty ghastly, isn't she? Harrington can certainly pick 'em. There's nothing worse than a respectable whore. Still, at least she's cleared. Incidentally, that's Sergeant Pritchard lurking in the corner. I've got him with me because he's the best man on the local drug situation.'

Furnival nodded to the plump, totally unimpressive figure. 'He's been in with you from the start,' he said to Calvert.

'Well, yes,' Calvert raised the eyebrow. 'Did you think you were teaching your grandmother to suck eggs? But have you got anything else for us?'

'I went to call Landseer off this morning.' Furnival told the two men of Landseer's beating up, and the questions that seemed to have touched it off.

'Anything that happens to Landseer's face must be a change for the better,' murmured Calvert. He made a note on a pad. 'All the same, I'll get the copper on the beat to keep an eye on his house. Anything else?'

Furnival confessed that he had visited Redmond, and related the young man's account of the death of his friend, David Summers. Calvert listened intently, and when he had finished did not rebuke him but turned to Sergeant Pritchard.

'Is that the picture you got, Pritchard?'

'Yes, that's pretty much the same story.' The sergeant spoke for the first time. His voice was soft with a faint Welsh lilt. 'There was never any reason to tie his death in to the Birdcage. And the picture we get of the club is just as your nephew says, Mr. Furnival. Kids take pills, some smoke pot, but they pass them around between themselves, the management never seems to be involved.'

'They wouldn't take the heroin there, would they?'

'Not unless they were desperate for a fix. They go somewhere private. Marihuana smoking is a social act, taking heroin is a lone act.'

'What would they need if they did fix at the club? What is the stuff like?' asked Furnival.

'On a prescription it would be in tablet form, one sixth grain tablets. In bulk, if the stuff was smuggled in, it's a white crystalline powder. It's sold by the gramme, and it is almost always heavily adulterated with lactose, sugar, baking soda, or something of that sort, to multiply the profits. It can be sniffed like snuff, but addicts fairly soon advance to injection. They dissolve the tablets or powder in a little water in a bottle, or even a teaspoon, by warming it over a match or lighter. Then they draw the liquid into a hypodermic syringe, or, if they don't have one, an eye-dropper with a hypodermic needle taped to it will do. They inject the stuff under the skin, or, if they are on to 'mainlining' for maximum results, into a vein.'

There was a grim silence. 'But there has been no smuggling from abroad?' asked Furnival.

'Two or three abortive attempts. Chinese sailors at Liverpool, I believe. They came to nothing.'

'The groups would be a perfect way of moving the stuff about,' said Furnival, remembering something that Gino had said. 'Travelling from one end of the country to the other with their instruments. Playing to thousands of kids in dance halls in big cities and ports. A perfect cover.'

'We thought of that,' said Calvert. 'In fact it's been done more than once with cannabis — it's been found packed in guitars and drum kits. But not in this case. There are five or six young chaps in some of these groups, too many to keep their mouths shut. We've hauled several of

164

them in to question them about the
Birdcage, and I'll swear they are innocent.
And I don't think any of them are on
drugs. In fact they say Leslie is very
adamant about not employing drug
addicts.'

'So all we could charge him with at the
moment is permitting his premises to be
used for smoking and trading cannabis,'
went on Calvert. 'It's not enough, not
nearly enough. Now if we could tie him in
with Barbara's murder . . . '

'He had Landseer attacked,' suggested
Furnival.

'Would Landseer swear to it? No, not
even to you. In any case that needn't
have any connection with Barbara, it
could have been simply chastisement for
curiosity.'

'He threatened me over the telephone,'
said Furnival. 'My wife took the call. He
said I was to 'lay off, or he'd have me
worked over like Landseer'.'

'But your wife doesn't know his voice,
does she? Just assumption again, you see.'

'Does he have an alibi for Barbara's
murder?'

Calvert took a little time answering. He pulled a note pad towards him and started to doodle tiny stick men on it.

'Well, the extraordinary thing is that he hasn't,' he said at last. 'It's so extraordinary that it almost suggests innocence. Mr. Leslie is a very glib boy with his alibis. Oh, he'll come up with one, I could see the brain cells working on it before I'd been with him five minutes. But the odd thing is, he wasn't ready with it.'

'Is anybody alibied?'

'Only Miss Smith.' Calvert doodled some more. 'You know this is an odd case, Furnival, if we forget Harrington and concentrate on the Birdcage people. It was strange that she wasn't killed in her own room, but *why* was she killed at all? She wasn't becoming a nuisance like Summers. She wasn't nearly that far gone, she was good for months, if not years, more custom. Had she discovered the truth about Summers' death or a drug ring? She doesn't seem to have been the type to care. She didn't even know Summers. So what was the motive?'

There was a pause. 'If I can help in any

166

way,' suggested Furnival gently.

Calvert regarded the last little man he had drawn. He added a skirt and wriggles of hair. 'Did the girl fancy you?' he asked.

Furnival stared. 'The girl?'

'Dinah Merriman, Leslie's girl. Don't tell me you haven't met her.'

'I've met her, yes.'

'Well, did she seem to fancy you?'

'Not that you'd notice. What do you have in mind?'

'I thought you might work on her a bit — you know, informally. Soften her up.'

'Redmond has been working on her for six months.'

Calvert made a scornful gesture. 'A kid! But a good looking man of the world . . . I'd do it myself, but she knows who I am. You could work incognito.'

Furnival looked from one detective to another. Sergeant Pritchard grinned at him.

'Go on, Mr. Furnival,' he said. 'When did you last get an assignment like that!'

11

Furnival left Calvert's office with some-what mixed feelings. It looked as though, after a dozen years on the Force, for the first time his life was going to resemble that of the detectives who strode purpose-fully through television dramas. He was conscious of a mixture of excitement and foolishness, the last because he more than half suspected that the London detectives were making a fool of him.

As he drove towards Avery Street an idea was forming in his mind. What if he should take a room in the house? Elaine would not be sorry if he moved out. It would distract Leslie and his thugs from Manorleigh Court, and Furnival himself would be right in the centre of things.

But negotiations would have to wait until morning. He would have to discuss it with Joanna, and he did not think even Mrs. Marshall would rent a room at after ten o'clock at night.

He turned the corner into Avery Street and at once spotted Dinah Merriman in the light of a street lamp descending the steps of the house to a bright pink mini that stood at the curb. She wore a leopard skin coat and black boots that disappeared beneath it.

Furnival whizzed the car up to hers and stopped within a foot of it. He leapt out as she turned to look back enquiringly her hand on the mini door.

'Oh, Miss Merriman, you're going out! And I was just going to take you up on that drink.'

Dinah Merriman paused uncertainly. 'I was going to work.'

'*To work?*'

'Yes. I'm a dancer at a discothéque. Didn't you know?'

'How would I know?' Furnival attempted a glance that he hoped combined supplication with the right degree of worldly charm. 'I'd love to see your act.'

The girl did not crumple at his feet but she still hesitated. 'Well, I have to go right now, I'm very late. You can follow on if you like. The Birdcage in Alder Court.'

She curled her thigh-booted legs into the mini, revved up furiously, and the bright little car leapt forward. Furnival jumped back into his own car and followed, keeping Miss Merriman in sight with difficulty as she darted in and out of the traffic. When the car entered Alder Court it turned down a narrow lane that Furnival had not noticed on the previous night, and through double wooden gates that stood open. Inside the gates there was a large yard, very dark except for one lamp above a small door. Furnival could see piled boxes and drums and the usual junk lying around, in addition to two or three cars, one of them large, white and opulent. Dinah Merriman got out of her car, locked it and walked out to Furnival in the lane.

'I'm sorry you can't park in here. Just staff, Mr. Leslie is very fussy. You'll have to back out and park on the main street. See you inside, right?'

'Right,' said Furnival. He fumbled long enough to see her disappear through the small door in the yard and backed down to Alder Court.

When he arrived at the club on this occasion there was no guardian at the door and he was able to walk straight in. The room was much less crowded than on the previous night. The music was supplied by a fairly subdued record player. The protoplasmic lights still blobbed about the walls. Furnival leant against the wall and looked the clientele over. He could see none of his limited circle of acquaintances, and no one took the slightest notice of him.

He made his way to the bar, bought a whisky, and, returning to the main room, found a table in an uncrowded corner. He sat and drank the whisky while he pondered on the foolishness of his actions. He was aware that every bright notion that entered his head had probably been discarded by a team of very experienced detectives months earlier. Mr. Leslie was no amateur, he had got to Landseer and to Furnival's telephone number within hours. It looked as though he was going to end up with nothing but a dented skull and a lighter pocket.

The arrival of Dinah Merriman interrupted his train of thought. She slipped into the seat opposite him, smiling nervously. She looked beautiful in a high-necked, sleeveless white dress, but tense and uncomfortable, quite unlike the relaxed, confident girl he had spoken to in Avery Street.

'I'm sorry,' she said. 'No act tonight. The group have left early and I don't like performing to records.'

Furnival looked disappointed. 'I'm sorry, too. I was looking forward to it.'

Dinah started to get up. 'Well, perhaps some other time.'

'You're not going? But what about our drink?'

The girl's eyes darted from side to side. She's being watched, thought Furnival.

'I'd like that,' she said. 'But not here. This is just for kids. I know a swell place quite close by.'

'But I rather like this place,' said Furnival. 'It's different. Let's have one here before we go on.'

The coloured girl looked at him with

something close to despair in her eyes. Then she stood up and flicked her fingers towards the bar. The bartender immediately materialized in the doorway, threaded his way around the edge of the room and took their orders. It was the first example of room service Furnival had seen in the place. He said so to his companion.

She gave a tight smile. 'I thought you hadn't been here before.'

Furnival struck his forehead with his fist.

'Christ, I'm a great detective! You're right, I was here last night. I thought your dancing was marvellous, I had to see you again.'

'Why did you come here last night?'

'I was asking about Barbara Jayne, remember? Someone told me she came here.'

Their drinks arrived and the barman left without waiting for payment.

Dinah picked up her martini and twiddled with the cherry stick.

'What did you say your name was?' she asked.

'Matthew. Matthew Furnival.'

'That's nice. I like that very much. And you seem like a nice man Matthew. I wish you'd get out of here.'

'Why? I'm only having a drink. You must have some very touchy playmates, Dinah.'

'Can you wonder that they're touchy? The least little thing that happens around here brings the police crowding in like flies. As soon as one of these stupid spineless kids gets into any trouble they start hounding Mr. Leslie.'

'They are only kids, Dinah. Don't you think they need some protection?'

'I was on my own from when I was fourteen years old. No one ever looked out for me.'

'But people are different. You had a lot of looks and talent and self confidence. Not everybody has. But we don't have to quarrel, I'm not hounding your Mr. Leslie, and I have no further interest in Barbara Jayne.'

'Are you off the case?'

'Yes, my client was cleared.'

Dinah sipped her drink and looked at

Furnival thoughtfully. 'Was your client Harrington, that middle-aged jerk who used to date Marian Smith?'

'That's right.'

'And the police have cleared him?'

'That's right,' said Furnival again.

'Who else is there? Not Marian?'

'She has an impeccable alibi.'

Dinah's eyes widened. 'Not Leslie? They're not thinking of Leslie for that?'

'I don't know what they're thinking.'

'They must be crazy. I know the police are longing to get something on him, but not that. Why should he kill her, he scarcely knew her?'

'Mr. Leslie and his friends can play very rough.'

'That's different. He doesn't go around strangling girls.'

'Are you sure?'

The girl suddenly drained her glass and sprang to her feet, her whole body tense with panic. Furnival thought she meant to flee and caught her wrist, but she only signalled again to the barman and subsided slowly into her chair.

'He hardly knew her,' she said again as

though reassuring herself. 'I told him about the murder at lunchtime yesterday — he couldn't place her for a moment. He was surprised to know we lived in the same house. Look, Matthew, I know men — it's my business — I know when they're lying. The murder was news to him.'

Furnival became aware of the barman standing beside the table with a refill of drinks regarding him inscrutably. He shoved money towards the man who silently withdrew.

'Leslie's reactions weren't exactly innocent,' he said. 'He had a colleague of mine savagely beaten-up, he had me followed, he telephoned threats to my wife.'

'That was nothing to do with Barbara's death. There are — other things. Nothing very bad, but he doesn't like people nosing around.'

'What sort of things, Dinah? What sort of things doesn't Leslie like people nosing around?'

'Nothing very much, I told you. Nothing serious.' Her long dark eyes flashed sideways in fear. 'Please stop asking me questions, Matthew. You'll get me into trouble.'

'Oh, aren't you inviolate? Might your lovely face be smashed in? Could you be strangled, too?'

This time the girl did start from the table. Furnival grabbed her arm and pulled her down again. 'Tell me, Dinah, I'll see no harm comes to you. And if it's really nothing, no harm will come to Leslie.'

Dinah hesitated. Then she said in a voice so low Furnival could hardly hear it, 'Well, there's pot, for one thing, cannabis. Mr. Leslie doesn't supply it, but a lot of the kids smoke it here. It's against the law, it's one of those ridiculous laws nobody takes any notice of, but it carries a ten year maximum sentence, and if the police could prove it against Leslie they'd stick him with it good and heavy.'

'And you regard it as harmless.'

'Sure it is. Less harmful than tobacco. People have been smoking it all over the world for hundreds of years. I've been smoking it for ten.' She smiled seductively. 'I think you'll agree I'm in pretty good physical shape.'

'But Dinah, this is not a country of lotus eaters sitting around in the sun trying to forget their empty bellies. This is a harsh northern clime, a sophisticated industrial economy. A man has work and responsibilities, he can't alternate between flying and lethargy. It doesn't suit us, unless you're aiming to produce a race of drop outs.'

Dinah looked sullen. 'We don't do anyone any harm. God, you ought to have met some of the boozers I've known!'

'Yes, I know all those arguments. O.K., we'll leave pot. What about heroin?'

'I know nothing about heroin. Pot is our scene, we leave 'horse' to whitey.'

'Did you know Barbara was on heroin?'

'No, I didn't.'

'Ever see any sign of it around here?'

'I told you, no. I'm doing all right. I mind my own business.'

There was a long silence while they drank their drinks.

'Why don't you say 'you can go now',' said Dinah. 'You've got all you wanted, haven't you?'

'I haven't got anything,' said Furnival.

Dinah stood up. 'So long, copper,' she said coldly. Furnival finished his drink slowly. He could not spot Leslie or any of his staff, and yet he still had the strong sensation of being watched. The music from the record player stopped suddenly, and the arrival of half-a-dozen young men with a large collection of electronic hardware announced that a live group was about to go into business. The lights in the room went up, and a faint spark of animation rippled through the audience. Furnival who had been about to embark on a quiet tour of inspection, cursed the brighter lighting.

A young girl stopped alongside the table, stooped down and kissed him firmly on the mouth.

'Hello, Dad, you still here, then?' she said. It was his young friend of the previous night.

'I have been home since,' said Furnival. He wiped his mouth. 'And don't go around kissing strange old men. I'm afraid I forgot your name.'

'You didn't get it. You palmed me off

on some grotty kid. It's Trisha.' She plopped down in the seat beside him.

'I was just going,' said Furnival. 'It's nearly midnight.'

'So what? The night is young. Aren't you going to buy me a drink?'

'Shouldn't you be going home?'

'What for? I don't need much sleep. Life's too short to waste in bed.' A banshee wail from an amplifier above their heads drowned her next words. She looked over at the group, busily arranging their gear with the precision of a neurosurgeon.

'Might as well go home,' she said. 'This lot are terrible.'

'Who are they?'

'The Fruit and Nuts. They're just a stand-in group. They have them when they can't get anyone else.'

'Where are the — er, Zebra Zodiacs?'

'They were here earlier. They left about half-past-nine to go up to Liverpool.'

'To Liverpool? Are you sure?'

'Yes.' The girl laughed. 'Not thinking of going up to catch their act, are you?'

'I wonder if they play there a lot.'

'Oh yes. Mr. Leslie's got a second club there. They sort of commute.'

Furnival said goodbye to the girl and slipped swiftly through the crowd to the door. There was no one outside in the passage, but there were two other doors, one near the street entrance, and one at right angles to the door of the main room. He tried this one first. It opened on to a short dead end corridor with two further doors, Ladies and Gents. Furnival opened the door of the Gents. It was bare and not very clean. Apart from the essentials it contained three wash basins with a gas water heater over each. Four of the shabbiest chairs from the dance hall had been brought in. He bent down and examined the floor. He found half-a-dozen spent matches. Here was the water and the matches that could be used while injecting drugs, but, although the provision of chairs was a little unusual, there was nothing that did not have a perfectly reasonable place in a men's convenience. He lurked in one of the lavatories for ten minutes but nobody came in, and he decided to try the other door.

The remaining door alongside the street entrance opened on to a staircase that turned a corner after a few treads. Furnival crept cautiously up to a landing where four doors faced him. The floor was carpeted in cheap brown sisal and the doors were varnished. There was not even the rather tawdry glamour of the public rooms. He listened, holding his breath. There was no sound of life, and no light under any of the badly fitting doors. He tried the door nearest to him. It was locked. So were the next two, but the fourth handle turned and the door swung gently inwards. Furnival hesitated. He had a strong feeling that someone was up on this floor with him, someone who had doused the light, and perhaps locked the door, when they heard him open the lower door. Was it likely that the club and bar should be in full swing with at least a hundred customers, and no one in charge except the barman? Landseer had said there were usually 'several young blokes' hanging about.

He stepped into the room and lit a match. It appeared to be a store-room used mainly for bar supplies; crates and cartons were piled on all sides. There was a little light from the window which overlooked the street. He lit another match and prowled round the shadowy blocks of merchandize and old accoustic equipment, prodding at some of the boxes. It was a good place to hide, but by the fourth match he was sure that no one else was there. He withdrew and quietly closed the door. He was about to descend the stairs when he noticed a door at the end of the passage where the light from the dim bulb barely reached.

Furnival opened the door and found a narrow staircase. He went down it until he reached another door at the bottom. He had a sensation of cold air penetrating from outside. He opened the door and had about three seconds to take in the littered back yard, the lamp above the door, the flash of strawberry and white cars, before something struck the back of his head with a sickening crunch and the ground reeled up to meet him.

<h1 style="text-align:center">12</h1>

Perhaps because of the awkward way he had been standing, still half inside the doorway, the blow did not render Furnival entirely unconscious. He was aware of someone lifting him under the arms, grunting with the effort while they did so, and dragging him across the yard. Then he heard a car door open and he was roughly hauled and bundled onto the back seat.

He tried to open his eyes, fighting off waves of nausea that swept over him. There was very little light in the car and he found it difficult to focus, but there seemed to be two figures kneeling over him rummaging through his coat.

One of his assailants suddenly gave a gasp.

'Christ, he's a copper!'

'Let me see that.'

There was a rustle of paper. 'The boss never said nothing about him being a copper,' muttered the first voice. 'I'm not roughing up any copper. You can get a long stretch for that.'

There was a pause. 'I don't think the boss knows he's a copper,' said the second voice. 'What the hell's he doing here, anyway? This says he's from Meddenham. Where's that? Has the boss got anything going there?'

'Shouldn't think so. He's got some cash here. Sixteen quid.'

'Better not touch it, and don't leave any dabs on that wallet.'

'What are we going to do?' The first voice returned to its theme. 'I'm not roughing up no copper.'

'The boss says we got to frighten him off before Andreas gets in.'

'I don't care. That's not my line of work.'

A face suddenly peered close into Furnival. 'I think he's coming round. Give him another little chop.'

'No!'

'Go on! You're supposed to know how to do it. And for Gawd's sake, don't croak him!' The speaker grabbed the front of Furnival's jacket and dragged him towards him. A stunning blow on the back of the head brought complete oblivion.

★ ★ ★

'Excuse me, sir. You're not thinking of driving that car, are you?'

The voice was quietly reasonable. Furnival looked up into the steady blue eyes of a young constable. He glanced around him, wincing at the sickening pain in his skull. The cold clear light of early dawn lit the squalid aspect of Alder Court.

He groaned and tried to focus on his watch.

'It's five o'clock,' said the constable. 'You've been making a night of it.'

'No.' Furnival struggled into a sitting position. He realized he was at the wheel of his own car, and it was exactly where he had parked it on the previous night. 'No, it wasn't what it looks like.'

The policeman smiled from a wealth of experience.

'You haven't been drinking?'

'No. Well, yes, I had two small whiskies.'

'Have you got any identification, sir?'

Furnival found his wallet and handed it over. As he did so he noticed that the contents had been roughly disturbed.

'Perhaps you'd better be careful of fingerprints,' he said. 'Two goons just went through it, but I expect they were careful.'

The policeman looked at him in surprise, and took the wallet gingerly.

'Detective-Inspector Matthew Furnival, Meddenham Division,' he read. He looked at Furnival again. 'I'm very sorry, sir. I'm Lewis. Were you on a job? Did you run into trouble?'

'A modicum, Lewis, just a modicum. Tell me, could I have been here for five hours?'

'Oh, no. I pass this point every twenty minutes. You weren't here twenty minutes ago.'

'I was coshed soon after midnight.'

'Where, sir? Not in the Birdcage?'

Furnival looked at him sharply. 'What do you know about the Birdcage?'

'I've been told to keep a special watch on it.'

'Yes, it was at the back of the Birdcage.'

'Do you want to make a complaint?'

'Good God, no. At the moment I want to get home. My wife will be worried sick.' Furnival peered in the driving mirror and saw a rather greenish face with a smear of oil on one cheek and a red abrasion on the other. 'On the other hand I don't feel up to driving. Do you think you could get me a lift?'

'A patrol car should be passing the end of the street any minute. I could flag it down.'

'Good man, Lewis.' With the constable's help Furnival got out of the car and managed to stay on his feet. 'If you want to put in a report about this you'd better mention Superintendent Calvert, he'll know what has been going on.'

'Yes, sir, what about your car? Do you want us to tow it in?'

'No, leave it here. It will give me an excuse for coming back again.'

Half an hour later Furnival was ensconced on Elaine's settee with Joanna bathing his face, and the three Harringtons leaning over him anxiously.

'You said we were going home this morning,' said Joanna for the third time. 'You promised me you wouldn't have anything more to do with it. Oh, Matthew, how could you? You might have been killed.'

'I'm sorry. I did intend to give it up. But when I went round to see Calvert last night he suggested a line of enquiry.'

'That's why we didn't worry as much as we might have,' put in Nicky. 'Aunt Joanna telephoned Calvert at midnight and he said he knew what you were probably up to, and to ring him again if you weren't home by this morning.'

'Oh, did he? Well, I assure you I wasn't "up to" anything he has in mind.' Furnival pushed aside his wife's ministrations and sat up. 'Joanna, I would like to stay for a little longer. I have a feeling things are coming to a head. I had an idea last night,

I could get a room in Avery Street, there should be one empty.'

'In the murder house?' breathed Nicky.

Furnival glared at him. 'It would keep any trouble away from here, and I'd be right in the middle of things.'

'Oh, no, Matthew,' wailed Joanna. 'I should want to know you were safe. He can stay on here, can't he, Elaine?'

'I don't actually think there is a lot of danger,' said Furnival. 'Not to me, and certainly not to you. Leslie's boys eased off as soon as they found out who I was. I get the impression his best efforts are directed against helpless kids and wash-outs like Landseer.'

'Stay here as long as you like,' said Gerald. 'You dropped everything to come when I was in trouble.'

'Well, we'll see,' said Furnival vaguely. He got to his feet and made for the bedroom. 'But right now I'm going to get a couple of hours sleep.'

Furnival's couple of hours stretched into four, and it was ten o'clock before he was washed, shaved and breakfasted. He took a second cup of coffee to the telephone, and dialed the number Calvert had given him.

'Well, well, well, Furnival. I've been getting the oddest reports about you,' Calvert's voice was mocking. 'Picked up drunk and disorderly at dawn!'

'Do you want to know what really happened?'

'Go ahead.'

'Is it all right over the 'phone?'

'I always assume so. How did you make out with the lady?'

'I think I was resistable. I talked to her for an hour at the club. She was insistent that her friend is innocent, just sensitive. All the same she's scared of him.'

'Anything else?'

'Not really. She gave me the legalize pot bit, you know, it's less harmful than alcohol.'

'You can skip that, I know it by heart. Then what?'

Furnival broke off to wave to Elaine and Joanna who were sallying forth to visit Elaine's 'darling little boutique'.

'Then I searched the place,' he said returning to the phone.

'You *what*?'

'Well, I had a look around.'

'Mr. L. didn't object?'

'He didn't seem to be there, or his henchman. In fact the place seemed to be deserted. But his car, and Dinah's were still there. I didn't find anything, needless to say. When I got outside into the yard somebody coshed me.'

'Badly?'

'I feel a little fragile. I think they must have given me a whiff of something. I wouldn't have been out five hours from that blow.'

'I wonder why they kept you in the place for five hours?'

'Perhaps till the lump went down. Or until they could get instructions from L. They weren't very efficient anyway. I got the impression it was amateur night. What was the point of the exercise? Not to prevent me searching the place, I'd finished searching, I was on my way out. And not to identify me. L. already knew my name and where I was staying when he telephoned my wife. They didn't know I was in the police, that gave them a bit of a shock.'

'Nice somebody still respects us. What were they like? Could you see?'

'Not very well. Certainly not to recognize them again. They weren't very big, they had trouble dragging me across the yard. I think they were both dark, and I'm pretty sure they were young.'

'That doesn't tell us much. Mr. L. has half-a-dozen pretty young gentlemen working for him. What were their voices like?'

'I got the feeling they were of foreign extraction.'

'You mean they had foreign accents?'

'No, they had cockney accents. But there was something in the rhythm of their voices, and the way they pronounced 'Andreas' that suggested foreign origin.'

'Andreas?'

'I was going to tell you about that,' Furnival changed position on to his other haunch. 'They said, 'the boss says we got to frighten him off before Andreas gets in'. Mean anything to you?'

There was a pause at the other end of the line.

'Not a thing,' said Calvert.

'I thought it could mean a ship docking.'

'Could be.'

'I suppose you know L. has a second club in Liverpool, and his groups commute between the two?'

'I knew he had a club there, yes.' Calvert seemed suddenly distant. 'Well, thanks a lot for your help, Furnival. What were you thinking of doing now?'

'I have to pick up my car from Alder Court sometime.'

'Oh, of course. I'm afraid you're going to have a hefty parking bill. Wish I could put you down for expenses, but I don't know how I'd enter you!'

'How about 'STOOge',' suggested Furnival coldly.

He replaced the receiver irritably. He was convinced that any collaboration between Calvert and himself was going to be very one-sided. He looked up as Nicky drifted into the room from his bedroom.

'Nicky, what does Andreas suggest to you?'

'Toilet paper,' said Nicky promptly.

'No, what kind of person?'
'A waiter.'
'Oh. Anything else?'
'A foreign waiter.' Nicky slumped at the table and started buttering cold toast. 'Why? Did you encounter one last night?'

'I heard of one. Did you know Leslie ran another club in Liverpool?'

'Yes, it's called Amidships. I believe it's a real groovy joint, I thought of going up sometime.'

'Well, why not?'

Nicky looked at his uncle, toast poised half way to his mouth. 'Did you have something in mind? I have a distinct feeling I'm being cast in the Doctor Watson role.'

'This group, the Zebra Zodiacs, do you know any of them?'

'Yes, I know one or two of them pretty well.'

'Would you say they are villains?'

'Hell, no! They're as gentle as doves.'

'I hope you're right. I don't want you getting into any trouble.'

'What do you have in mind?' asked Nicky again.

'How do they travel?'

'They have a van, an old Bedford.'

'My idea was that you miss the train back from Liverpool and scrounge a lift with the group.'

'And then I overpower them all and search the van?'

'No, you just play it by ear. Keep your eyes open. See if anything unusual is loaded on, or if anything is unloaded en route.'

Nicky thought it over briefly. 'O.K., I'm on,' he said.

'You're sure you don't mind?'

'It'll be a pleasure. Anything's better than work.'

'Right, all we have to do is find out exactly when they are playing, and when they're likely to leave.'

'That's easy. There are always posters up in the Birdcage about the activities at the Liverpool club. I'll have a look in on them today. Then I'll go to the last session and hang on until the group is ready to leave.'

'That's fine. But Nicky, for God's sake, be careful. Don't try to be a hero.'

'Don't worry, I'll do my Wodehouse act.' Nicky smiled at his uncle with touching confidence. 'You'd never believe how stupid I can seem when I try!'

13

Furnival left his nephew warming to his expedition, packed a small case with essentials, and took the Tube to Avery Street. He decided to postpone collecting his car until later when there might be some life around the Birdcage.

He was disgorged from the mouth of the Tube station a short distance from the house and walked the length of the quiet street enjoying the sunny, blustery morning. At number twelve he mounted the steps, waved a cheery hand at Mrs. Cobbett's curtains, and rang the bell.

After a few moments Mrs. Marshall appeared and greeted him without enthusiasm.

'It's no use you coming to me with any more questions, Mr. Furnival. I've told you everything I know, and I've work to get on with.'

Furnival smiled ingratiatingly. 'I

haven't any more questions, Mrs. Marshall. I've no more interest in the case now that my brother-in-law has been cleared.'

'Oh, has he? Well, I'm sure very glad for you. Though I never really thought a gentleman like him would have had anything to do with it. I've just been cleaning out his young lady's room, not that there's much to do, she's left it very nice.'

'She's moved out, has she?'

'Came and cleared all her stuff out last night. Reckon that's the last little romance for her! It's left me with two empty rooms,' she said, playing into Furnival's hands.

'As a matter of fact that's why I called,' he said. 'I need a room for a short time, and I thought your house looked so very pleasant when I called before, I wondered whether I might rent one from you?'

The woman looked doubtful. 'Well, I don't know. It would have to be Miss Smith's. Nobody has shifted Barbara's things yet.'

'Miss Smith's room will be fine.'

'It's ten pounds a week.'

'That's a bit steep. After all — with a murder in the house,' said Furnival meanly.

'Well, eight then. I can't go less than that. In advance.'

'Can I move in now?'

Mrs. Marshall agreed and Furnival moved past her up the stairs. On the first floor she flung open the doors to the bathroom and lavatory, unlocked the door of Marian's room and handed him the key ring.

'There you are, it's all ready for you to go in. No unreasonable noise, and no lady friends to stay all night. There's a shilling-in-the-slot meter for your fire, but I pay for your light so don't burn it too late.'

Furnival closed the door behind her, and surveyed his home-from-home. It was comprised of one very large room with two sash windows overlooking the street. One corner was divided off by free-standing shelves to serve as a kitchen-cum-dining-room furnished with cupboards, table and chairs and a small cooker. The rest of the room was the bed-sitting area, with divan bed, wardrobe, dressing-table, easy chairs and a modern electric fire. The furnishings were adequate, but not sumptuous, and for a love nest it was hardly inspiring. No sign remained of Marian Smith's brief tenancy.

He walked over to the large rug near the door where he supposed Barbara's body had lain, but it held no message for him.

He picked up the keys from where he had dropped them on the bed. There were three on the ring, one Yale key, presumably for the front door, and two, slightly different, room keys. And two room keys might mean that Mrs. Marshall had not given him Marian's keys but her own bunch. He cautiously opened the door and looked up and down the staircases. There was no sight or sound of anyone.

He slipped across the landing, turned one of the keys in the lock of Barbara's door, and pushed it gently open. The room was fundamentally very similar to the one he had just left, but, still garlanded with Barbara's personal belongings, it gave the impression of being totally different. The bed was unmade, and was strewn with discarded underwear and cuddly toys. A line supporting stockings had been stretched across the kitchen section, and clothes hung behind the door to a depth of two feet. There was a film of dust, much more than three days accumulation, on every surface.

Furnival wrinkled his nose in distaste and set to work. He didn't expect to find anything that the police had not; all he wanted was to build up a clearer picture of the dead girl. He looked through the kitchen first which yielded nothing but the not surprising conclusion that Barbara had been an appalling housewife. He moved into the bedroom and opened the wardrobe. There were not many clothes in the wardrobe, but the entire surface of the inside of the door had been covered with pictures of pop singers, film stars and television personalities. Furnival was mildly surprised. He realized that such interests were common in the early teens, but Barbara, after all, was twenty years old and should have been coming to terms with real life.

He moved on to the dressing-table. The top was littered with the squalid remains of lipsticks, cotton wool, tubes and jars. He pulled open the two drawers, again there was not much in them, Barbara obviously believed in dropping her clothes where she took them off, but what they did hold was wildly untidy. Furnival rummaged through the not-too-clean undies, handkerchiefs, scarves and sweaters, and emerged hopefully with a large rose-painted tin such as might once have held biscuits.

He carried it to the bed, cleared a space to sit down, and prized off the lid. The tin was full to bursting with photographs, correspondence and newspaper cuttings. With a spark of excitement Furnival started to sort them into piles. At the end of an hour he had gained nothing except the insight into the girl's character he had sought. The photographs were all of celebrities, the newspaper cuttings concerned their doings and the chit-chat of their world. The correspondence all related to self improvement courses of the most superficial kind. Teach yourself to dance, cultivate a fascinating personality, become a model. This last course had cost seventy guineas and negotiations had swiftly dropped. There were coupons for 'trial offers' of every imaginable commodity from false hair-pieces to bust developing creams. There was a large collection of autographed programmes from pop concerts. There was not an item that could have been called personal. The girl seemed to have lived on dreams. She had an obsession with the trivial that was almost heartbreaking.

Furnival gently packed her treasures away and took stock of the room. Of course the police would have taken away anything they regarded as important, including her hypodermic and supply of drugs if they had been in the flat. He realized he had missed the drawer in the bedside cabinet and he opened it now. He was faced by another jumble of contents, a magazine, a comb and mirror, aspirins, and hand-cream. He pulled the drawer out completely, it was lined with a piece of flowered wallpaper. Furnival lifted the corner of the paper and a photograph looked up at him.

One photograph, one single photograph among this mass of mementoes. He looked at it curiously. It was a carefully posed snapshot of a young woman sitting in a garden with a baby on her lap and a small boy leaning against her knee. It was an old photograph, apart from the brownish tinge it had acquired he could deduce that from the woman's dress and hairdo. The dress, he believed, was in the fashion known as the New Look, which had seemed so wildly romantic in his first schoolboy courting days and looked so curious now. The woman was fair and pretty and complacent looking, the baby on her lap was fair and pretty too. It was wearing a dress and was presumably female. It appeared to be about nine months old. The small boy had dark hair and eyes, and was about three years old. Furnival was convinced that he had seen him in the last few days. He would now be in his early twenties. He carried the photograph across to the window and looked at it for a long time, but could not place the face. His last few days had abounded with good-looking dark young men, Terry from Gino's, his tail in the National Gallery, the collection from the Birdcage. It seemed a reasonable assumption that the baby in the picture was Barbara with her mother and brother, photographed, perhaps, by proud papa.

Furnival hesitated for a moment then put the photograph away in his wallet. He left Barbara's room and locked the door. He was beginning to regret involving Nicky in a mission that could be highly dangerous, and he determined to call him off at the earliest possibility. He ran down the two flights of stairs and was relieved to notice a telephone in the hall. He rang the Harrington number for some seconds but got no reply.

Furnival walked the half mile to Alder

Court attempting to rationalize his worries. He had at least until teatime to call Nicky off, he was unlikely to set out before that, and perhaps not for a day or two if the Zodiacs were playing several nights.

He turned into Alder Court, located his car, and walked on to the Birdcage. The club looked even more shabby and uninviting by daylight. The neon sign was out and the dusty front door was shut. Furnival could dimly see the piled crates behind the uncurtained window of the first floor store-room.

He found a small Italian restaurant close by and ate an excellent lunch. He was undecided what to do next. Rob, Dinah, and the Birdcage, were not available to him, and he did not feel inclined to inflict himself on Calvert. He fetched his car, and, when he was pretty sure he was not being followed, set out for Landseer's flat.

Landseer's bruises had already almost blended in with the general wear and tear of his face, and he looked remarkably healthy tucking into a plate of ham sandwiches and a glass of beer.

He greeted Furnival warmly, and fetched a second glass and bottle.

'How's the detective business, Mr. Furnival?'

'Slow, Landseer, slow.'

'I'm glad you've come.' Landseer subsided heavily back into his chair. 'I may have something for you.'

Furnival looked at him in surprise. 'You? Why, you haven't been outside, have you?'

'Not likely. That little darkie has been running all my errands. No, I have a marvellous invention over there.' He gestured towards the corner. 'It's called the telephone!

'I sat here all day yesterday with my split lip and my bumps hurting like hell, and I got madder and madder. People ought not to go around beating up helpless old men! So I started ringing up a few of my old contacts.'

'Any luck?' asked Furnival, pouring his beer.

'Well, of course, my narks don't have much to do with the new breed of villains, but one or two are on the fringe of both worlds, and one told me that Leslie doesn't hire his help by paying them big money, but because he's got some sort of hold over them.'

'Do you mean they're drug addicts?'

'Oh no, they wouldn't be reliable enough. But this man says he has a couple of Pakis who got into the country illegally, and an American soldier on the run from the Vietnam draft.'

'But how does this help us?'

'It doesn't yet. But my nark reckons this Yank is a real nice kid who detests Leslie and all he stands for. If we can get hold of him and sort of appeal to his better nature — you know how idealistic Americans are — he'll very likely tell us everything he knows, and perhaps do a bit of spying for us as well. This bloke thinks he's just about ready to break.'

'Can we get hold of him?'

'He hasn't been around for a few days, but my friend will try to get him over here as soon as he turns up.' Landseer folded a substantial sandwich into his mouth.

'Now, tell me what you've been up to, Mr. Furnival.'

Furnival recounted everything that had happened, while Landseer chewed and nodded.

'I don't know if you were wise giving out that Mr. Harrington has been cleared,' he said when Furnival had finished. 'Leslie probably felt confident when he thought the police had somebody else.'

'I didn't want him to feel safe. I thought if he was rattled he might do something stupid.'

'He might also do something vicious. It's a good move as long as nobody is wandering around at risk.'

Furnival told him about Nicky going to Liverpool and his fears for him.

'He'll be all right with the group. I'm pretty sure they're O.K. And I don't think they'd shift heroin in the van. They might move cannabis from Liverpool in it, but not heroin.' Landseer ruminated for a moment. 'And you say Dinah Merriman thought Leslie was clear of Barbara's murder?'

'I hardly know her, but she was very convincing.'

'And he wasn't ready with his usual alibi? That's certainly odd. But if not Leslie, who else? You say Miss Smith is alibied. That only leaves us your brother-in-law with the conventional motive that Calvert likes so much, Rob Redmond, and Dinah, and it's hard to think of any motive for them.'

'I keep thinking,' said Furnival. 'Why in Marian's room?'

'Could she have been looking for something? Drugs, perhaps? Did this Marian look like a junkie?'

'Emphatically not, although she might drive someone to them!' Furnival took out the photograph he had found in Barbara's room and passed it to Landseer.

'Have a look at this.'

Landseer adjusted a pair of spectacles on his nose and studied the photograph. 'Old-fashioned,' he said. 'Just after the war, isn't it? Never saw the woman around here.' He looked at it a minute longer. 'The little boy looks familiar.'

'That's what I thought.'

Landseer shook his head. 'Can't put a name to him, but I'll bear it in mind.'

'Thank you, and for all other help. And if your young American turns up get me over right away.' Furnival stood up and took from his pocket a bottle he had acquired in the restaurant where he had lunched. 'I brought this along to speed the convalescence.'

Landseer grasped the bottle tenderly by the neck.

'Grapes!' he said. 'How thoughtful of you.'

Furnival left Landseer and drove back to Avery Street. He found a multi-storey car park in the vicinity, left the car, and walked to the house.

Inside, he went at once to the phone in the hall and rang the Harringtons' flat. Elaine answered him.

'No, Matthew,' she said, in answer to his query. 'Nicky isn't here, but he left a message for you.'

Furnival's heart sank. 'Read it to me, will you, Elaine?'

'He says he's catching the four o'clock

train to Liverpool, and to tell you that it has to be tonight because it's a one night stand. What does he mean, Matthew?' Elaine's voice rose shrilly. 'What is Nicky up to?'

14

Furnival looked down at his watch. It was ten minutes past five. So Nick had left, for better or for worse, and there was no way of stopping him. He had managed to reassure Elaine, telling her that Nicky was merely going to make some quite harmless enquiries, and told her that he intended to spend the night at Avery Street.

He trudged up the stairs his legs as heavy as lead. Last night was beginning to take its toll. He unlocked the door of his room, took off his shoes, and lay back on the bed. Within five minutes he was fast asleep.

He was awakened by a slight sound near the door. He sat up quickly. The room was almost dark. There was a faint and most attractive perfume in the room. Dinah Merriman left the door and came and sat on the bottom of the bed. She regarded him sadly.

'Furnival, you are a nut. You move into this house, you lie there sleeping with the door unlocked . . . What's the matter with you, don't you like living?'

'I was too tired to get up and lock the door. But I'm safe with you, aren't I? You assure me Leslie is innocent.'

'Somebody killed Barbara.'

'Who?'

She shrugged. 'How should I know.'

'Redmond?'

'You're crazy. That kid!'

'So you've no suggestions?'

'Look for someone who loved her.'

'Redmond loved her.'

'Not enough. Not in that way.'

Furnival's eyes grew accustomed to the dusk. He saw that she was wearing a tightly belted coat in dull gold velvet that shone and slithered sensuously as she moved.

'What time is it?' he said.

'Nearly eight, I'm on my way to work.'

'Dinah, why do you work for Leslie?'

She laughed harshly. 'Oh, God! You're not going to try to convert me, are you? What's a nice girl like you doing in a place like this? How corny can you get! Listen, Matthew, dear, my line of work isn't ever going to take me into any Sunday schools, and it's the only thing I'm any good at.'

'There are better places than the Birdcage.'

'Then I'll move on to them sometime. At the moment I'm doing all right where I am.' She took two cigarettes from a gold case and threw one to him. 'What makes you the people's conscience, anyway? I'll bet you're not even getting paid.'

Furnival leant on one elbow, smoking and regarding her thoughtfully. 'Where did you get to last night, after you left me?'

'I went out to have some supper.'

'Where did you go?'

'Angelo's, it's a few doors down Alder Court.'

'Yes. I know it. Do they open so late?'

'They open till midnight. Why? Do I need an alibi? What happened?'

'Nothing to indicate Leslie's innocence. If you don't already know, I was sapped by a couple of his goons coming out of the back of the Birdcage.'

She stubbed out her cigarette. 'It's private property, you shouldn't have been there.'

'I'm aware of that. But there are more conventional ways of warning people off.'

'You probably tripped and banged your head. Those stairs aren't very safe.'

'They hauled me into Leslie's car and frisked me. I heard them talking.'

Her head came up sharply. 'What were they saying?'

'Oh, they were quite talkative, they thought I was out. Leslie doesn't employ a very high grade of help.'

'What were you looking for anyway?'

'I was looking for you.'

Dinah suddenly slid up the bed and lay down beside him. He turned and saw her dark eyes gleaming inches from his.

'You're the real police, aren't you, Furnival?' she said.

'Yes.'

'I knew you weren't any old hack gumshoe like Landseer. You're too professional.'

'I never felt less professional in my life.

I'm just blundering around in the dark.'

'How do you come to be involved?'

'Gerald Harrington is my brother-in-law. His wife thought he could use some help.'

'In-law trouble, huh? I had my share of that once.'

'I didn't know you'd been married.'

'It was a long time ago. I was seventeen years old. He had golden hair, and loads of charm, and a public school accent. I worshipped him. You can imagine how his mother took to me.' She smiled ruefully. 'But I got him in the end. It took mama nine months to break up the marriage, but by then I didn't care. I'd found out he was a sadistic drunken bum. It's not easy to tell with Englishmen, you know. England really does breed the most charming bums. I think that's partly why Mr. Leslie appealed to me. No one could ever mistake what he is.' She rolled over on her elbow until her face was very near to his and ran her fingers gently across his cheek and mouth.

'Or what you are, Matthew,' she

whispered. 'It would be very easy to fall in love with you.'

Furnival caught at her fingers, and tried to draw away. 'No, Dinah.'

She stared at him. 'It isn't my colour, is it?'

'You know better than that. You're the loveliest colour I've ever seen. But I have a very pretty wife just half-a-mile away I could go to bed with if that was what I had in mind.'

'But it isn't?'

'It's getting to be more so every minute!' He dropped her hand and sat up. 'Did Leslie send you here?'

'Nobody 'sends' me anywhere.'

Furnival stood up and switched on the light.

'I'm going out to get something to eat. Will you come with me?'

Dinah got up off the bed slowly, and smoothed her hair. 'No, I told you, I have to go to work.' She made for the door without looking at him. As she passed him Furnival stopped her. 'Dinah, you say that Leslie is innocent. Who do you think killed Barbara?'

She paused in the doorway. 'I think it was Harrington,' she said. 'I think it was your brother-in-law.' She went through the door closing it gently behind her.

After she had gone Furnival felt restless and unsettled. He opened the window irritably to let out her haunting perfume, went to the bathroom, and washed. He put on a clean shirt and a jacket, and went out into the cool, damp evening. He was not hungry, but it was a long time since he had eaten, so he looked around for a café. He began to enjoy the walk, and went farther than he needed. He found a coffee bar in a quiet street, ate hamburger and chips, drank two cups of coffee, and set off to return home. On the way he bought a notebook at a bookshop whose stock would have given the Meddenham Watch Committee apoplexy.

Back in Marian's room he pulled the table beneath the feeble light, and settled down with notebook and pen to try to bring some order to his impressions. He struggled with it for over an hour, sorting out relationships, alibis and statements, before he admitted to himself that he was getting nowhere, and that he could concentrate no longer. He was desperately sleepy after the long walk in the fresh air, and he kept wondering how Nicky was faring. He put away the notebook and prepared for bed, carefully locking the door this time. He was glad to note that Marian's bed was extremely comfortable. The last thing he saw before he fell asleep was the face of a small boy, pretty and maddeningly familiar, in a faded old photograph.

He awoke the following morning depressed and debilitated after a restless night haunted by strange and vivid dreams. The same theme ran through them all. He was in a dense jungle where the sunlight filtering through the leaves made blobs of gold which pulsed and throbbed over the dark foliage. The light would not keep still but dazzled him as he vainly tried to push through the undergrowth. Then suddenly there was a trench like an open grave in front of him, and in it lay Barbara, in the flimsy kimono she wore in the autopsy photographs, but with her face smashed and unrecognizable. There was a low laugh behind him, and a flash of gold, like Dinah's velvet coat or the dress she danced in, vanished among the trees. Then all the faces came from behind the trees and advanced menacingly towards him. Leslie and the Ape and all the pretty young men, Calvert, Rob and Gino, Dinah and Marian, all pressing in on him until he broke out in a cold sweat and was suffocating and could not cry out. At one point he thought he put a name to the child in the photograph but the answer was not possible.

It suddenly flooded in on Furnival that there had been no message from Nicky yet. It would be characteristic of Nicky to contact him as soon as possible to recount his adventures. It was now nine o'clock. What could have happened to him? The concert would end at three o'clock at the latest, and the drive back to London should not take much more than four hours. Furnival's spirits sank lower and he groaned aloud.

He got out of bed and prowled miserably around the room. He realized that he had neither tea nor coffee and he did not feel inclined to start the day without some fortification.

He washed, shaved and dressed, and went upstairs to the second floor. He listened outside Dinah's room but there was no sound. He admitted to himself that he wanted to see her in a quite disturbing way. He hastily tapped on Redmond's door and was answered by a muffled grunt. He opened the door and looked into the room. Once again Redmond was in bed, but he looked rather healthier than on the previous occasion, and the room was noticeably tidier. He goggled at Furnival in surprise.

'Not you again? You choose some bloody awful times to call.'

'It's a personal call. I live here now.'

Redmond sat up and scratched his tousled head.

'Since when?'

'Since yesterday morning.'

'Where? I mean which flat?'

'Miss Smith's. I'm afraid I overlooked my housekeeping. Can I borrow some tea or coffee and some milk? I can't face the day without them.'

Redmond got out of bed and went to his kitchen, still staring at Furnival incredulously.

'Well, if you aren't the funniest cop I ever met! Are you sure you are a cop?'

'I was until three days ago, I'm getting less sure all the time. Where were you yesterday?'

'Out looking for a job. Very worthy, eh?'

'Commendable. I thought you might be doing a spot of detection.'

'I'm not looking for trouble. I've got my own life to lead.' Redmond emerged from the kitchen holding two tins. 'Which do you want, tea or coffee?'

'It doesn't matter.'

'The tea is less ancient, better have that. And you can have this milk. It's yesterday's but it doesn't pong too much.'

Furnival took the offerings. Redmond went back to bed and pulled the bedclothes over his head. 'Close the door on the way out,' he said.

Furnival returned to his own room, and made and drank his tea. He lit a cigarette and returned to his notes which now at least appeared to be a little more rewarding. At eleven o'clock there had still been no call from Nicky and he decided that he must take some action. He left the house, retrieved his car, and drove to Alder Court.

He parked the car some distance from the Birdcage and walked back. Like yesterday, the club was shuttered and appeared deserted. He walked on to the narrow lane that Dinah had driven up. The wooden gates to the parking lot of the club stood open, and from it he could hear loud cries and shouts. He hurried forward and looked into the yard. There, kicking a football about, and looking as sweet, innocent, and reasonable as children were four young men. Furnival recognized them with a flood of relief. They were collectively the Zebra Zodiac.

They saw him watching them and stopped their game.

'Looking for someone, mate?' one called.

Furnival advanced into the yard which, apart from one old black Ford, was empty of cars.

'I was looking for my nephew, Nicky Harrington,' he said. 'He went up to hear you playing in Liverpool last night. He was going to hitch a lift back in your van. I wondered if he had got back yet.'

'The van isn't back yet,' said a tall, skinny, ginger-haired youth. 'We were wondering where it had got to, it's usually here by now.'

Furnival's heart plummeted. 'Why — don't you drive down with the van?'

'No, we come down by train, get a bit of kip. Mr. Greenaway loads up the van and drives it down for us.'

Mr. Greenaway. It had a reassuringly Victorian ring. 'Mr. Greenaway,' he said feebly, 'I don't think I know him.'

'Of course, you know him,' put in a chubby-faced dark lad. 'Everybody knows Mr. Greenaway, he's always around the Birdcage. Built like a prize fighter — or a gorilla. In fact most people call him the Ape.'

15

From somewhere Furnival collected his reeling senses. 'Did you see Nicky?' he croaked. 'Did he ask for a lift?'

'Yeah, we were talking to him for a while,' said the ginger-haired one. 'He asked if we could bring him back, and I said to go to the dressing-room after the show and see Mr. Greenaway. I wouldn't like to make any promises for Mr. Greenaway, he's not always very friendly.'

A handsome lad in flared trousers and bright felt poncho laughed shortly. 'And that's putting it mildly!' he offered.

Furnival's scalp crawled. 'Did you see Nicky after the show? Do you know if the Ape — I mean Mr. Greenaway — did give him a lift?'

The gaucho shook his head. 'No, we have to beat it pretty fast to catch the train. Mr. Greenaway and the staff at Amidships load up our gear.'

'Does Greenaway always drive the van?'

'Yes, we can't drive.'

'What, none of you?'

'No. Funny isn't it? Shep and Don here haven't learnt, and Pete is too young.'

'And you?'

'Aw, I was disqualified. A technicality.'

'Driving at seventy down a one-way-street,' guffawed the ginger-haired lad who seemed to be Shep.

'And the van is late?' asked Furnival.

'Yes, he's usually here before now.' Shep looked kindly at Furnival. 'Look, are you worried, mate? Would you like us to ring Mr. Leslie, and see if he's heard anything?'

'No,' said Furnival hastily. 'No, but thanks a lot.' He walked back down the lane to Alder Court. At least it was clear now how the movements of the group could be utilized without involving the boys, simply by using non-driving players, and persuading them that travelling by train would be more restful.

He spotted a telephone box on the street corner, went into it, and rang the

Harrington flat. He waited impatiently while it rang for some moments, but there was no answer. He put down the receiver, hesitated for a minute, then rang Calvert's number.

Calvert was a long time coming to the phone and when he did he sounded preoccupied.

'Ah, Furnival, I'm rather pushed for time, I'm afraid.'

'So am I. I think I may have landed my nephew, Nicky Harrington, in some trouble.'

'Forgive me, but is it my concern?'

'Yes, it is.' Furnival threw discretion to the winds and plunged in. 'Nicky travelled up to Liverpool last night to hear a pop group play at a club called the Amidships. He intended to hitch a lift back with the group. This group also plays at the Birdcage.'

There was a pause. 'And now, not surprisingly, he has gone missing. Was this your bright idea, Furnival?'

'Yes, it was. But I thought — everybody thought — that the group was clean.'

'And they're not?'

'It's worse than that. They don't drive themselves. The Ape drives the van, they travel by train.'

'What — always?'

'Apparently.'

'Hm, that's rather interesting.'

'I don't care how interesting it is, Nicky has to be found!'

'But Furnival, would he have been idiotic enough to go off with the Ape?'

'I don't know, I wouldn't think so, on the other hand he's bored, foolhardy, eager to help — '

'In a word, his uncle's nephew. Christ, Furnival, are you all like this down at Meddenham? It must be a real madhouse. The very last thing I wanted to do was alert Leslie that I was watching him.'

'I'm sorry, I knew you'd be annoyed.'

'We can take that as established. How late is the van?'

'The boys just said it was late. He drives through the night.'

'Well, I'm not going to put out an alert yet. No, shut up and listen! It could be against young Harrington's interests to do so, he may still be fooling them somewhere. I'll have a man quietly watching the club and Leslie's place at Richmond. Not that he goes in for any dirty work there. It's just after twelve. Keep in touch, and if there's still no sign of him by two o'clock we'll go into action. And Furnival, no more bright ideas, please!'

Furnival rang off. He had been spoken to like a naughty schoolboy and he more than deserved it. He got into the car and drove soberly to the Harringtons' flat. It seemed as good a place as any to await developments. He hoped that Elaine was still out, but when he mounted the stairs at Manorleigh Court, there she was, opening the front door of the flat, a bag of groceries on her arm and smiling happily.

'Hello, Matthew, are you going to stay to lunch? I left Joanna window-shopping up west, but I thought I had better dash back and get a meal for Nicky.'

'Elaine,' said Furnival. He stopped wretchedly.

'Yes, Matthew?' She looked at him enquiringly. Then, behind his back, the bedroom door opened, and her eyes changed to the doting expression that could only mean one person. He turned round. In the bedroom door, sleepy and rumpled but quite unmarked, stood Nicky Harrington.

'You woke me up,' he said aggrievedly.

'Nicky!' Furnival surpressed an impulse to hug his nephew. 'Where have you been? I rang you.'

'Oh, was that you? I put my head under the bedclothes. I was trying to get some sleep. I've had a jolly tiring night.'

'You bloody fool! I've got the Metropolitan police alerted over you.' He leapt for the phone, got Calvert on the line, and explained the situation. He bowed his head humbly beneath the Superintendent's lurid suggestions, and rang off.

'Matthew! What does this mean?' Elaine was squeaking. 'If you sent Nicky into trouble last night, I'll never forgive you.'

'Mama, darling, why don't you go into the kitchen and get us some lunch?' suggested Nicky. 'Uncle Matthew is looking rather low, and I have a tale to unfold that I think might upset you more than somewhat.' He led his mother towards the kitchen, came back and draped himself along the settee smiling complacently at Furnival.

'Seriously, Nicky, you might have rung me,' grumbled Furnival. 'I've just made an awful fool of myself with Calvert.'

'But I *did* ring you, as soon as I got back here. No one answered, and I was just dropping on my feet, so I got into bed and I must have fallen asleep right away. It would be about a quarter past nine when I telephoned.'

'I was up in Redmond's room about that time, it must be impossible to hear the phone from there. Well, never mind now, tell me what happened last night. I know that the Ape and not the boys drives the van. You can imagine how that grabbed me!'

'Just try and imagine how it grabbed me! I spent a ghastly five hours, drinking coke and listening to that bloody music, trying to decide whether to be a hero or not. The Zodiacs told me to go and square it with Mr. Greenaway, so I'd taken a peep to see who Mr. Greenaway was! Well, in the end I thought there was no harm in asking, just to see how he'd take it.

'I thought at first he was going to refuse. He stared at me for about five minutes, it was rather unnerving, you could see his primitive little brain churning over. Then he said O.K. I could come along if I helped him to load up the van.'

'You helped load the van?' broke in Furnival eagerly.

'I did. The group cleared off at two o'clock, but it was some time before we could get everybody out of the place, and there was a lot of stuff to load up, so it was nearly three before we left.' Nicky broke off as Elaine came in with two cups of coffee.

'Well?' prompted Furnival.

'Nothing. I'd swear nothing came out of that hall that didn't go in. There were lots of people helping, and nobody supervised what you took, you could pick up anything and take it out. The Ape just saw that it was properly stacked and wouldn't get broken.

'When everything was loaded up I went to get in the cab, but the Ape came up and put a hand like a sandbag on my shoulder, and said in his hoarse voice, 'No, get in the back and go to sleep, I don't want you rabbiting away in my ear all the way to London.' Well, the feeling was mutual, and anyway when the Ape says get in the back, you get in the back! I crawled into a space in the back and lay down, and after a reasonable interval I commenced what I hoped were convincing light snores, while I poked and prodded around among the instruments.'

'Any luck?'

'Not a thing. But listen, Uncle Matt, when we had been driving for twenty minutes, he stopped. He looked over at me to make sure I was asleep, then he got out. After a few minutes he came back with another man. They talked for a little while, I couldn't hear what they were saying, and then he opened the back of the van and they put two tyres in.'

'Tyres?'

'Car tyres. The other chap let out a yelp when he saw me, but the Ape shut him up. He said I was asleep, and I was stupid even when I was awake, and it was a good thing to have a witness that he hadn't fetched anything from the club.'

'Were those his exact words?'

'Yes.'

'And you say he'd been driving for twenty minutes when he stopped? He would have been clear of Liverpool by then, in the middle of the night. Have you got a road map?'

'It was exactly twenty minutes, I looked at my watch. But I think he was circling around until I went to sleep.'

'You think you were still in Liverpool?'

'Yes, or on the outskirts. And I know the name of the street. I peeped out when the Ape went to fetch the other man. It was a narrow cobbled street of stores and warehouses, and I could see a street nameplate, it was called St. Clement's Way. We were stopped in front of a small garage with two petrol pumps. I had the feeling we were near the sea. I could smell it, and it was cold and damp.'

'Nicky!' exclaimed Furnival. 'You are a genius! I think we are on to something.

We've definitely redeemed ourselves. What small backstreet garage is open at three in the morning for any legitimate purpose?'

'But Uncle,' broke in Nicky. 'That isn't all. When we were under way again I felt inside the tyres. They were packed all the way round with paper packages!'

The rest, of course, was all anti-climax. The Ape had made no further stops, and had dropped Nicky 'without even a goodbye', out by the North Circular Road at eight o'clock. Nicky had caught a bus and got home by nine when he had tried to ring his uncle.

Furnival thanked his nephew warmly. 'At last we've got something concrete for Calvert, and just let him raise his eyebrows at me this time!' He went to the phone and made an appointment to see Calvert, who was out, as soon as he returned.

'Do you know any other groups who play the Birdcage?' he asked Nicky. 'There was a bunch called the Fruit and Nuts on the night before last, do you know of any others?'

'There's a group who stand in occasionally called the Red Shadows, they do a sort of *Desert Song* send-up, burnouses and palm trees and stuff.'

'Could you locate any of them?'

'I expect I can find someone who knows where they hang out. Of course they may be at the other end of the country, they get about, you know.'

'Yes, that's what I was thinking of. Will you get hold of a member from both groups and ask them one question? Ask whether any of them can drive.'

Elaine came in at that moment to announce lunch, caught their self-congratulatory mood and forgave Furnival. Joanna, arriving laden with shopping, was delighted at how placidly her husband took her extravagances.

'By the way, Nicky,' said Furnival as they adjourned to the kitchen. 'Did I tell you that I'm extremely angry with you for being so reckless?'

16

Furnival and Nicky arrived at the police station promptly at three o'clock for their interview with Calvert. It was a meeting to which Furnival was looking forward, but when they presented themselves at the desk the sergeant informed them that Calvert had left hurriedly half-an-hour before.

'But he was expecting me,' protested Furnival. 'I have something extremely important to tell him.'

'I'm sorry, sir,' the sergeant led them to a small waiting room near Calvert's office, and politely pulled out chairs for them. 'I know the superintendent wants to see you, but something came up suddenly. He went out of here like a bat out of hell. if you'll pardon the expression. And he said would you kindly wait?'

'Certainly, sergeant.'

'Would you care for a cup of tea, sir?'

They declined the tea. They sat on the

hard wooden chairs and examined the bare office, and when they had exhausted that, they discussed again every detail of Nicky's Liverpool excursion, the case in general, and possible reasons for Calvert's sudden exodus.

At four o'clock Furnival stood up and stretched. 'Well, it had better be good! We've been here for an hour. I've a good mind to take that sergeant up on his tea.'

He turned round as the door crashed open. Superintendent Calvert stood in the doorway looking about seven feet tall and in a towering rage.

He spoke to Furnival with precarious self-control. 'Come into my office, Furnival. I want to speak to you. No, alone, Harrington can stay here.'

Furnival followed Calvert in bewilderment. He noticed Sergeant Pritchard and two other plainclothes men whispering with the desk sergeant. They all turned to look at him.

In his office Calvert shut the door and faced Furnival.

'Furnival,' he said icily. 'Are you stark raving mad? I ought to report you for what you've done.'

'For what I've done? You mean sending Nicky Harrington to Liverpool. I know it was stupid and irresponsible but it turned up some solid results — '

'I'm not talking about that. I'm talking about breaking into the Birdcage last night. Leslie complained to the police!'

'What a bloody cool nerve!'

'Be that as it may, he's within his rights and he's pressing charges. By God, this is a bitter pill for me to swallow. I told you he'd got me once for wrongful arrest. He stood there and laughed at me. And what a rotten, unprofessional job to make of it, it looks as though a hurricane had hit it, his property smashed — '

'I didn't disturb a thing,' protested Furnival. 'Wait a minute, did you say *last night?*'

'Yes, last night between eight and nine o'clock.'

'Well, you'll be relieved to know it wasn't me.'

'*It wasn't?* I hope you can prove it.'

'Oh, yes, I can prove it. I have a cast-iron alibi. But why were you so sure it was me?'

'You were too quiet all day,' grinned Calvert. 'I was sure you must be up to something. And who else would be fool enough to go after a bash on the head two nights running! I'm very sorry, Furnival. And I'm afraid I was rude to your nephew. I'll call him in now.' He turned at the door. 'About that alibi, is it really foolproof? It will have to be good to get Leslie off our necks.'

'It's good,' said Furnival. He did Calvert's eyebrow trick with great satisfaction. 'Just tell him I was in bed with his girl!' He enjoyed Calvert's expression before reluctantly enlarging on the circumstances.

Calvert left the room and returned with Nicky, his arm affectionately round his shoulders.

'Now, please sit down and tell me your story, Mr. Harrington,' he said. 'I'm sorry I was brusque earlier. I thought your uncle had pulled a boner but I should have known better!'

Nick recounted his escapade again, and Calvert listened attentively without interrupting. Then he took him back in detail over every point. When he had finished he looked at the notes he had made for a long time, then at Furnival.

'It will be cannabis,' he said.

Furnival felt an obscure pang of disappointment. 'Not heroin?'

'Almost certainly not. There was too much of it. And coming into Liverpool in tyres indicates cannabis. It comes over from Jamaica. It's too well known a route for heroin, they'd never risk it.'

'Is there much profit in it?'

'Not bad. The current asking price in London for a block of cannabis resin is four to five pounds. It would bring in a lot more broken down into individual smokes. There could have been a couple of hundred blocks in those tyres. You did a very courageous job, Mr. Harrington, I can't thank you enough.'

'Are you going to act on it?' asked Furnival.

'I must. I have to stop that cannabis being distributed. Don't worry, a professional trafficker on this scale could get ten years for cannabis alone.'

'It won't stop the heroin traffic.'

'What heroin traffic? Look, Furnival, we've never had a shred of real evidence to connect Leslie with heroin. And if he *is* involved he can't be taking receipt of his consignment if he's inside for a good long stretch!'

'Someone else will be only too happy to take receipt of it. It will only stop one end.'

'But what can I do? I have to try and find that cannabis, you know that!'

'What about Barbara's murder? Do you intend to charge him with that?'

'No. Don't look like that. Do you think I've been sitting idle while you ferret around? My men have been through Leslie's story with a toothcomb. He has a good alibi and he wasn't too glib with it. He was with two men of reasonable integrity at the time. To be honest, I would have liked another few days before this cannabis story broke. Like you, I have a feeling we might have pulled off something bigger. But it *has* turned up, and I must act on it.'

'You say Leslie has a good alibi,' said Furnival. 'What about the Ape? I never thought of Leslie doing his own killing.'

'The Ape was with Leslie at the time; he was driving him.'

'And he couldn't have gone back to Avery Street?'

'No, too far.'

'I'm sorry,' said Furnival. 'I shouldn't be trying to teach you your job.'

Calvert shrugged. Suddenly he looked very tired. 'I'm glad of help from anybody,' he said. 'But you must remember when you're dealing with professional criminals, there are a lot of things you suspect, but you know you will never be able to prove them.'

He went out into the corridor. Furnival and Nicky looked at each other feeling deflated. Calvert came back with the Welsh sergeant.

'Let's have your story through again, Mr. Harrington,' he said. 'We'll have it in the form of a statement this time.'

Nicky went through his story once more, and Pritchard asked a number of questions, none of which his superior had overlooked.

'I forgot to tell you before,' said Nicky.

'I managed to locate members of two other groups who sometimes play at the Birdcage. I telephoned them just before we came here. None of them can drive. Mr. Greenaway, as they call him, always drives their vans, and they take the train.'

'That's very significant,' said Calvert. 'Now I think the first thing to do, Pritchard, is to contact the Liverpool police. There shouldn't be any difficulty in locating the garage, and when they've picked up the fellow we'll get Harrington to go up and identify him. I want it done swiftly, before he has a chance to get in touch with any of Leslie's mob. And I want a check with the port authorities about recent arrivals particularly from the West Indies. Then, very discreetly, have a search made for those two tyres. You can fan out between where the Ape dropped Mr. Harrington off and the Birdcage, any unobtrusive garages, warehouses, sheds, anything of that sort. Find out if Leslie or the Blaikie brothers own any property in the area. Take as many men as you need. O.K.?'

'O.K. What will you do, sir?'

Calvert grinned. 'Are you being cheeky? I'll get over to the Yard, to the Drugs Department. They may already know something to tie in with this business. If they can give me even a shred of reason to hold off for a day or two, I'll do it.'

Pritchard moved to his own desk, spread out his various notes, and pulled the two telephones towards him. 'What about Mr. Leslie's complaint, sir. Do we go ahead and investigate it?'

'You bet we do. He wants coppers — fill the place with coppers. Give him coppers till they're coming out of his ears!'

Calvert said goodbye to Furnival and Nicky warmly, and escorted them to the door. They walked down the hall and out into the car park. They were getting into the car when the desk sergeant appeared in the doorway puffing slightly. He waved to them to stop, then padded up and put his head in through the car window.

'Superintendent Calvert just yelled out for me to stop you, sir. I think something has come in over the blower.'

Furnival and Nicky hurried back into the building at the sergeant's heels, and along to Calvert's office. They knocked, and he shouted to them to come in. He was sitting at his desk, staring down at the telephone in front of him.

'That was a call from Gino's,' he said. 'You remember Gino, that little pansy hairdresser where Barbara was employed? One of his assistants just went back to work and found him beaten up in the room behind the shop.'

'How bad is he?' asked Furnival.

Calvert's voice was harsh. 'The boy thinks he is dying,' he said.

17

They lost no time in setting out for Linden Terrace. Calvert with Sergeant Pritchard and a detective constable in a police car, Furnival and Nicky following behind. As they turned into the terrace they saw an ambulance standing outside Gino's shop, with a small crowd gathered around it. They got out to find the ambulance crew trying to manhandle a stretcher up the area steps, a portly well-dressed doctor directing the operation.

'Wait a minute,' shouted Calvert. He shoved his way through the knot of bystanders. 'Take him back inside, I want to talk to him.'

'Not a chance,' said the doctor with something like satisfaction. 'I've just given him a shot.'

Calvert swore. 'When is the earliest I can speak to him?'

'Perhaps in twelve hours, perhaps not.

He has a broken jaw, a broken cheekbone, a couple of ribs are almost certainly bust and they may have perforated a lung. He's a very sick man, and if his assistant hadn't found him he would have been a dead one!' The doctor raised his voice. 'Constable, can't you clear those bloody vultures out of the way?'

Calvert and Furnival watched the stretcher loaded into the ambulance, and the ambulance drive away. The crowd turned as one man to stare down at the detectives in the area.

'Let's go in,' said Calvert. 'We'll see if the boy can tell us anything.'

They entered the salon, Pritchard and the constable behind them. It was undisturbed, the tempting mirrors and the myriad bottles glinting in them were unbroken.

'No search,' said Calvert. 'Just chastisement. The Ape is back in town!'

Nicky blanched. They went on through to the small room at the back of the shop. This, too, was undisturbed. At Gino's desk John sat drinking the medicinal sherry from a large mug. His face was ashen, and there was a trace of blood on the cuff of his pale blue sweater.

'How are you feeling, lad?' asked Calvert kindly. 'A bit shaken up, I expect?'

'Oh, I feel terrible, Mr. Calvert. I'm shaking like a leaf. Who could have done such a thing to a little pet like Gino?'

'Yes, who — and why? Did he say anything?'

'He just — he could barely speak, his mouth and teeth were smashed,' John looked sick at the recollection. 'He just sort of moaned, 'they killed her, they killed her.' Then his mouth filled with blood, and he started to cry.'

'Nothing else?'

'No. Just 'they killed her', over and over again.'

'And you didn't see anybody around?'

'God, no.'

'How did you happen to be here? Early closing day, isn't it?'

'Yes, we finish at one o'clock on Saturday. But I met a friend who invited me for a day out in the country tomorrow. I particularly wanted to wear my new suede jacket, but I'd left it at work, so about five o'clock I popped along to pick it up. Gino is usually here, you see; he lives above the salon.'

'It's a good thing you did. He would very likely be dead if no one had found him until Monday morning.' Calvert turned to Pritchard and the constable. 'Don't stand idle, lads, have a look round here and upstairs. See what you can find.'

'John told me that Gino had quarrelled with Leslie,' said Furnival. 'A couple of months ago he refused to have him or his associates in the salon, presumably because of Barbara going to the club.'

'It wouldn't be a reprisal for that — too belated.'

'I wasn't thinking of that,' said Furnival. 'I believe it was Gino who broke into the Birdcage last night.'

'*Gino?* That's pretty unlikely, he's no hero.'

'Perhaps he is.' Furnival thought of the parchment-coloured face they had just seen on the stretcher, half hidden by gauze and dressings. 'He was very cut-up over that girl.'

'That girl, that girl!' shouted John hysterically. 'There's been nothing but trouble ever since she came. We never had a girl here before, what did he want to hire her for? She was nothing but a — ' He uttered an expression so filthy that even Calvert looked shocked.

'Now, now, that's enough of that! Pull yourself together. You haven't told me yet how you got in. Was the front door unlocked?'

'Yes, it was, and Gino was in here on the floor beside the desk,' said John sulkily. He smoothed a hand over his golden cap of hair. 'I'm sorry I flew off the handle, but it's a fact, Mr. Leslie was ever so charming until people started upsetting him.'

'And a good tipper too,' said Furnival.

John glared at him. 'Can I go now? I want to have an early night to get over this, before I meet my friend tomorrow. It's quite spoilt my weekend!'

'Yes, you can go now. Mr. Harrington, why don't you see John to his home, he's still a bit shaky?' Calvert watched the two young men down the passage. 'Don't forget the new jacket,' he called to John. He turned to Furnival.

'Pretty obnoxious water-fly, that. I hope you didn't mind my sending your nephew along with him, he *is* still a bit groggy, and, helpful though Harrington has been, I shouldn't let him sit in on police business. I wonder if you could be right about Gino breaking into the Birdcage, Furnival? I'm inclined to agree with you. And Leslie had decided to wreak his own rough justice without waiting for us.'

'I don't believe Gino knew or cared about the cannabis traffic,' said Furnival. 'There *is* something else.'

'Are you back on that again,' Calvert groaned. 'Well, did he find it? He couldn't have brought it here, or they would have taken the place apart looking for it; and surely Gino would have got in touch with us as soon as possible if he had found anything. It's over twenty hours since he did the club — if he did do it.'

'That young pouf said he was repeating that they killed her,' put in Pritchard. 'Wouldn't that imply that he had found some evidence?'

'Not necessarily,' said Furnival. 'He said that to me once before. He just meant that they had got her started on drugs.'

'He may have something,' said Calvert. 'But conjecture is pointless until I can talk to him. Meanwhile, I think we should play it very close to our chests. Where are you going to be domiciled tonight, Furnival?'

'I think I'll spend another night at Avery Street. How would it be if I talked to Redmond? I could try to get out of him whether he did the Birdcage. If he didn't, it really only leaves Gino.'

'Good idea, let me know what he has to say. But apart from that, no action. We'll finish up here, and get those other enquiries rolling.'

Furnival left them and returned to his car. He started for Avery Street, stopping on the way for a meal. He ate it without enjoyment, his mind running in circles, then continued home. It was seven o'clock, getting dusk, and a thoroughly depressing evening. He went on past his room to Redmond's door and knocked, but there was no reply. He returned to his own room, and got out his notes. The cannabis traffic appeared to be established, but there did not seem to be enough money in it, even with the legitimate profits from the two clubs, to attract a big time operator. Leslie had a lot of overheads and quite a sizeable staff, however small their cut he would find it hard to maintain his house at Richmond, a luxury car, and an expensive mistress, on the residue. And Calvert had said that Leslie was merely the front man for two more infamous criminals, the Blaikie brothers. Presumably they would expect a hefty chunk. Not enough to go round, decided Furnival.

He lay on the bed in the almost dark room letting his thoughts range over the last few days. Both he and Calvert seemed to be getting sidetracked from the fundamental question, who had killed Barbara Jayne? He tried to concentrate, but kept seeing before his eyes the effeminate features, immaculate hair, and small, white hands of Gino, that unlikely hero. It could easily have been Nicky, he thought with a shudder. He was about to get off the bed when there was a quiet tap on his door. He sat up with a start, he had heard no one on the stairs. Then he recalled that this was just the time that Dinah had visited him last night, and his heart lurched like a schoolboy's.

'Come in,' he called.

Two young men entered the room. Furnival could see in the light thrown from the fire that the first was Rob Redmond. There was a much slighter figure lurking behind him.

Redmond's eyes found him on the bed. 'I've brought Carl,' he announced simply.

'Put on the light,' said Furnival. He looked at the second youth. He was small and skinny, with pale, scrubbed looking skin, light blue eyes, and fair cropped hair. He wore blue jeans, and a donkey jacket that looked several sizes too big for him.

'Carl?' he queried.

The young man stepped forward. 'Carl B. Hunniker,' he said. 'Mr. Landseer said you wanted to see me.'

'Landseer telephoned while you were

out,' put in Redmond. 'He said he had Carl with him, and it was very important that you talked to him. So I went over to bring him here. We waited until it was dark.'

Furnival had entirely forgotten the American draft dodger Landseer had promised him. He turned to Hunniker. 'You realize the danger involved in talking to me? I was responsible for poor old Landseer being beaten-up, and another man was almost killed this afternoon, probably by your employer.'

'I know, Mr. Furnival,' said Hunniker. He had a strong Southern accent. 'Nobody knows better'n me what that guy can do. But I'm sick of it. I've had it up to here with Mr. Leslie. I don't care if they send me down for thirty years, I'll tell you everything I know.'

'How long have you worked for him?'

'About a year. I was stationed in Germany until we heard about the Vietnam draft. Then I skipped with four other guys. We were in Holland for a couple of months, then my buddy and I came on to London, the other three stayed in Holland.

'I lost touch with my pal soon after I got here,' he went on. 'He shacked up with a girl and didn't want to know me. When I met Mr. Leslie I was desperate, I'd got nowhere to sleep and barely the price of a meal. I met him at the Birdcage, I think a girl had taken me there, I forget who she was — just a pick-up — and she suggested I might do odd jobs for him.

'He came and sat at our table; he got rid of the girl and talked to me for hours. All about my problems! Gee, I was dumb, I thought he was a perfect English gentleman. He ended by advancing me ten pounds, and telling me to look in every evening in case he had any chores for me.

'And that's all I did for two or three months, just odd jobs, driving, taking messages. It was the easiest money I'd ever made. Then one night he sent for me and said he thought I ought to know what I was doing. It should be all open and above board between us, he said. The following evening a boy on his staff, called Chris, was going to break into a hospital dispensary. The Ape was going along as muscle, I was to be waiting with the car. Well, as I said, I was very dumb. I said 'what do you want to break into a hospital for? Most guys want to break out', or some feeble little joke. And he said, 'We've got to get some heroin.''

'Heroin,' said Furnival quietly and with great satisfaction.

'Christ, I was horrified,' went on Hunniker. 'Sure, I'd realized by this time that some of Mr. Leslie's deals were a bit crooked, but I hadn't figured on drug running.'

'What did you say?' asked Furnival.

'I said no, as forcibly as you can with the Ape breathing down your neck. I said I wouldn't touch it, rather Vietnam than that. And he said that wasn't the choice anymore, I'd been driving hash all over London for weeks, and when I'd waited for Chris and picked him up a few days before, he'd been breaking into a drug warehouse after heroin. He said I'd get ten years, sure as hell!'

The young American curled his meagre

frame up in the armchair. 'I couldn't face it, Mr. Furnival, I never had much guts. I knew I'd be extradited to the States, and some of our pens are sheer murder. So I went along with them, I drove and fetched and carried, and tried to turn a blind eye to what I was doing.'

'Go on,' said Furnival. 'We can fill in the details later.'

'The funny things was, as soon as he had laid his cards on the table, Mr. Leslie got real friendly with me. He used to confide in me. He told me that all he'd done was to set up as middleman. He knew that addicts sold dope to each other, and it broke his heart that they did it at little or no profit. So he took over. He bought their surplus when they needed cash for rent or a meal.

'The first thing he concentrated on was making new addicts. He'd always sell to a new kid just starting before someone who was really hooked. He forced addicts to enrol new recruits, often blackmailing them by withholding supplies.

'He knew that junkies were reluctant to go to a doctor, because he was legally

261

bound to attempt a cure, and, with minors, contact their parents. He knew that they would dislike the new treatment centres that were being set up displacing the old G.P.'s, even more.

'As soon as the G.P.'s were forbidden to prescribe he would be the only alternative source to the centres, and he had a perfect outlet in the Birdcage with a lot of kids already on hash.

'Of course once he had made his new addicts the problem was supply. He persuaded anyone registered with a doctor to get them to increase their dosage — a few doctors would grossly overprescribe — he paid them or bullied them into stealing and forging prescriptions. Then he started burgling hospitals, chemists shops, manufacturers. He cut all he did get — '

'Cut?' queried Furnival.

'Adulterated, with lactose or sugar, to make it go further. But it still wasn't nearly enough. It got out of hand. He had meant to create a market and he'd created a monster. After David Summers died he realized he had to have another source and that meant importing.'

'Tell us about David's death.' Redmond's voice was quiet.

'The Ape killed him,' said Hunniker. 'Mr. Leslie didn't mean it to happen, but Summers had been bugging him for weeks. So had a lot of other junkies, but Summers was the worst. And Leslie simply didn't have the stuff to go round. So he told Ape to rough him up a bit, to kind of teach them all a lesson. But you know the Ape, he just doesn't know his own strength, and Summers died.'

'You know that?' pressed Redmond. 'You could swear to it?'

'I overheard him telling the Ape to do him up, and I heard him bawling him out when he killed the guy. He was as mad as hell about it.'

'And then he knew he had to get a bigger supply of heroin?' said Furnival.

'Yeah, but that's not easy. You know very little gets into Britain. It took Mr. Leslie a few weeks to get things fixed up, then suddenly supplies got a lot easier.'

'Do you know where it came from?'

'No, I wasn't in on the job. But he's

had two further consignments since then. Now we're very low again.'

'Do you know where it's kept at the Birdcage?'

'In the back of a fruit machine, a 'one-armed bandit', in Leslie's office. It's out of order, but it's never sent for repair.'

'Carl,' said Furnival. 'You are gift from the gods. A witness to the heroin traffic, *and* to Summers's murder!'

'And when I set foot outside of here I'm dead,' said Hunniker soberly.

'Don't you believe it, I'll guard you with my life. You say supplies are running low again, do you know of any plan to replenish them?'

'Not for sure. But I had an unusual job for tomorrow. I was to go down to Southampton to meet a man off a ship and bring him back to the Birdcage.'

'A man called Andreas?'

Hunniker looked surprised. 'That's right.' He was about to go on when there was a light tap at the door. The three men looked at each other.

'Come in,' said Furnival.

Dinah Merriman stood in the doorway. She smiled at Furnival, then she saw Hunniker and her eyes widened in alarm. 'Carl!' she said. 'What are you doing here?'

18

Furnival moved swiftly to the door, closed it and leant his weight against it. 'He's here, Dinah, because he's got a lot more guts than you!'

'He'll need it. The Ape will kill him!'

'Not if I can help it. He's a witness to the fact that Leslie caused David Summers's death, and to his filthy trade in drugs. A trade deliberately and cynically built up — '

'He was in on it, too. He took Leslie's money,' Dinah spat. She pulled at the door handle helplessly. Furnival caught her around the waist. She swung round on Redmond who was standing watching them, his face wretched. 'What's with you, lover boy? Are you going to let this big jerk keep me here?'

Redmond spread his hands helplessly. 'He can't let you go, Dinah.'

'Ring the police,' said Furnival. Dinah renewed her struggles, her strong dancer's body twisting in his arms. '*Go on*, Rob, ring Calvert, from the hall.'

'No, no,' Dinah relaxed suddenly. 'Not the police. If there's one thing I'm good at it's knowing when I'm on the losing side. I guess that little runt has told you all you need to know.' She dropped into a chair and smiled up at the three men. 'Time for Dinah to move on.'

Furnival took a seat between her and the door. 'Yes, Carl has told us all we need, but I wish you would add your share.'

'Leslie only supplied a demand,' she said sullenly. 'So the kids could score in a nice gay scene instead of those dreary centres — always trying to dry them out, lowering their dose — '

'Leslie *created* a demand. And how can you talk about a nice gay scene? This wasn't pot — he was dealing in death.'

'Well, I never knew about the heroin. I don't like 'horse'. But I thought all you cared about was who killed Barbara Jayne, so you could clear your brother-in-law. Don't tell me you've persuaded Hunniker to pin that on Leslie?'

'It was all I was interested in to start with, I got involved in the rest.' Furnival turned to Hunniker. 'Do you know anything about Barbara Jayne, Carl?'

'Barbara who?'

'She was a young girl who used to frequent the Birdcage, a pretty blonde of about twenty. She was on heroin. She lived in this house, and she was strangled in this room four nights ago.'

Hunniker looked faintly alarmed. 'I never heard of her.'

'Do you think you would have known if Leslie had harmed her?'

'They usually talked freely in front of me.'

'Hard luck, Furnival,' Dinah crowed. 'Better get Calvert to bring along some cuffs for that nice respectable Mr. Harrington while he's about it!'

Furnival felt a momentary unease. 'Never mind that for now. Dinah, are you going to be missed at the club? Had you better telephone them?'

'We can't let her call them!' burst out Hunniker.

'I could stand by her to make sure she

didn't warn them. What about it, Dinah?'

'There's no need to call. I don't go in if I don't feel like it.'

'Good. Then we're all going to hear the rest of Carl's story, and then I shall get Calvert over here.'

'Oh, have a heart, Matthew,' said Dinah. She crossed to his chair and twined her arms around his neck. Her voice was a breathy whisper in his ear. 'Let me go before the police get here. I never had anything to do with Leslie's business. I'll write you a full statement, and get my things and get out.' Her lips touched his ear softly. 'I was thinking of moving on, anyway. I've had a great offer — '

Furnival gently released himself. 'I'm sorry, Dinah, but it's not my decision. Go and sit down, there's a good girl, you work too well at close quarters!'

Dinah returned to her chair and curled up in it, her face averted.

'Go on, Carl,' said Furnival. 'You were going to tell us about Andreas.'

'I have to meet him at four o'clock tomorrow afternoon in Southampton in a little café called the Frying Pan.'

'Have you ever been there before?'

'I've never been to Southampton before, but I've got directions to get to the café. It's near the docks.'

'And then what do you do with him?'

'I bring him to the Birdcage at eight o'clock, to Mr. Leslie's office.'

'You don't know that he's carrying drugs?'

'No. Mr. Leslie just said to escort him to London because he speaks very little English.'

Furnival turned to the girl. 'Have you heard of Andreas?'

'No,' said Dinah sulkily.

'I'm going down to ring Calvert,' said Furnival. 'He's the C.I.D. superintendent on the case,' he explained to Hunniker. 'You realize I have to hand you over to him?'

'Sure,' said Hunniker. 'I just want to get it over with. There's nowhere else I can go anyway.'

'Well, I'm sure he'll do all he can for you. Keep your eye on the girl.' He ran down the stairs. He was not sure of their ability to restrain Dinah against her will. Carl did not look strong enough, and Redmond's heart clearly wasn't in it. He braced himself for a tackle at the front door as he dialled Calvert's number. He was relieved to hear the superintendent's voice, the responsibility for all the information he had acquired was beginning to rest heavy on him. He explained what had happened and gave a résumé of what Carl Hunniker had told him. Calvert was as excited as his suave façade would allow.

'I'll come over,' he said. 'No — wait. You bring him here in your car, and don't let anybody see him. We don't want Leslie and his boys to know that he's sung. He's going to Southampton as planned tomorrow.'

'He may do that, but I don't think you'll get him to go to Leslie's office with Andreas, it's too dangerous.'

'That's a chance he'll have to take, mate. I want to get Leslie at the actual pick-up.'

'You've got enough on him now. You can't force Hunniker to do it, and I don't think he will.'

'He will. Just you bring him over here. If we get the stuff actually changing hands we won't have any trouble in court. And we'll stand a better chance of roping in Andreas' end of the business.'

Calvert rang off, and Furnival went back to his room. Dinah, Carl, and Rob still sat as he had left them, watching each other guardedly.

'We've made Calvert very happy,' he said to Carl. 'We're going over to see him now. I'll go out first and see if the coast is clear; you follow along fifty paces behind until we get to the car.' He realized that he had only Rob to leave in charge of Dinah. He looked at him doubtfully.

'Rob, I'm relying on you to keep Dinah here.'

'At least let me wait up in my own place,' said Dinah. 'Boy scout here can watch the door from his room. Honest, Matthew, I won't skip.'

'O.K. Up you go,' said Furnival. He watched her mount the stairs to the second floor, Redmond at her heels, with some misgivings. Then he went downstairs and out into the night. He looked up and down Avery Street; it was completely deserted. He set out for the car park without looking behind. He retrieved his car from the fourth floor; by the time he had got into the driver's seat Carl Hunniker materialized by the passenger window. Furnival let him in, and they drove in silence to the police station.

Calvert met them in the hall and escorted them to his office where Sergeant Pritchard and a constable Furnival had not seen before were waiting. There he had Carl go through his story in detail, taking him back over points again and again, and asking innumerable questions. When he was finally satisfied he handed him over to Pritchard to get it in statement form, and turned to Furnival.

'Well, this is marvellous, Furnival. Didn't I say Landseer was a great copper? And I'll take back all I thought about our country cousins! We've had a bit of news in from Liverpool just before you telephoned. They've picked up young Harrington's tyre supplier. He's well known to them, and he's got a brother and a lot of friends who work in the docks. They're busy sorting them out now.'

'Any word on where the tyres ended up in London?'

'Not yet, but we were going very discreetly at this end. In fact I think I'll call the boys off until Hunniker gets Andreas to the Birdcage. That's far more important.'

'You haven't told Hunniker what you've got planned for him yet.'

'No, but he'll be quite safe, we'll have him covered all the time.'

Calvert waited until Hunniker had signed his statement, then explained what he wanted him to do on the following day. Hunniker was at first alarmed but soon agreed to co-operate.

'Nothing can possibly go wrong,' Calvert assured him. 'I'll send my best tail to Southampton with you. He'll stay closer than a brother, but no one will notice him. And we'll plan a little surprise party for Mr. Leslie at the Birdcage. Let us know of any change of plan. Now, let me see, what are we going to do with you tonight?'

'He can come back with me,' suggested Furnival.

'No, I don't think we'd better risk that again, he mustn't be seen with you. It's either a night in the cells, or back to his own pad.'

'I'd prefer the cells,' murmured Carl.

'But I think you should be at your own place,' said Calvert. 'In case of any calls. Constable Mears will go with you, and Herring will relieve him tomorrow and go to Southampton with you. Thank you, lad, and good luck!' Calvert put out his hand and Carl shook it, then followed Mears out of the office.

Furnival watched them go. 'I wouldn't want anything to happen to that boy,' he said. 'He's got nerve, he knows what these people can do.'

'I agree.' Calvert's face was grim. 'We'll look after him as well as we can. Herring is a very good man, but you can never promise one hundred-per-cent safety. Things can go wrong.' He picked up Carl's long statement, and started to read it through, while Furnival perched on the edge of his desk and smoked a cigarette. When Calvert had finished the statement he looked up at Furnival.

'No knowledge of Barbara,' he said.

'No.'

'I'm getting carried away. I keep forgetting that's what I'm supposed to be investigating.'

'I know, I feel that way myself.'

'Even dead, she has a way of making herself insignificant. Haven't you any ideas? I take it you still won't buy Gerald Harrington?'

Furnival hesitated. 'I have a sort of an idea at the back of my mind. Things have been too hectic to think it out.'

'Well, out with it, for God's sake, we don't want any more harm done.'

Furnival shook his head. 'No, it will keep until after tomorrow. Believe me, it's perfectly safe. No more harm will be done.'

Calvert looked at him. 'All right, I'll accept that.' He picked up a phone. 'I'll contact Herring to give him his orders, then I'll get everything laid on for tomorrow night. I suppose I can expect to see you at the Birdcage about eight?'

Furnival grinned. 'What do you think? In at the death.' He said good night to the silent Sergeant Pritchard and left the station. A distant clock struck eleven as he left the car and started on the short walk to Avery Street. He let himself into the house and went up to the first floor. A thread of light shone under the door of his room. As he reached the landing the door opened and Redmond came out. He looked at Furnival and swallowed hard.

'You're not going to like this — ' he began.

Furnival pushed him aside and looked past him into the room. It was empty. He grabbed Redmond by the lapels and shook him.

'You let her go!' he shouted. 'You stupid bastard, you let her go!'

'Furnival, I'm sorry. I couldn't help it. She didn't know anything about what had been going on, you could tell that. I couldn't keep her here.'

Furnival released him with trembling hands. 'You bloody fool,' he said again. 'She'll warn them. They'll kill Hunniker.'

'What? What do you mean? Hasn't Calvert got him at the station?'

'No, he let him go home. He is to go through with the meeting with Andreas as planned.'

Redmond sat down on the bed. 'Oh, my God! I'd better ring Calvert and tell him to call it off. He'll have to pick Carl up.'

'I don't think he'll do that,' said Furnival. 'His heart is set on this showdown.' He collected his thoughts. 'Did she say where she was going?'

'No, she just packed a few things — Furnival, I don't think she'll go near Leslie. She knows when she's on a losing wicket. I'm sure she just meant to blow.'

'How sure are you? Sure enough to gamble Hunniker's life? Oh, well, I'm not being paid to worry about it. We'd better go down and let Calvert know.'

They made the telephone call and, as Furnival had expected, Calvert was livid. Over the phone he reduced Redmond to an apologetic mess, but he was still determined that things should go on as he had planned.

When he had finished with Redmond he spoke to Furnival again. 'I'm inclined to agree with Redmond, I don't think that girl will go near Leslie. In any case I'm still going on with it. I'll assign a second man to watch Hunniker as soon as he and Herring get to London, and we'll watch out for any unusual moves from Leslie.'

He rang off. Furnival telephoned to Joanna to reassure her of his safety. Then he and Redmond went back up to his room, where they drank tea and talked in a desultory fashion until well into the night.

Furnival woke at nine the next morning after a few hours of disturbed sleep. He bathed and got some breakfast, then sat down before his notes again. He got out Barbara's treasured photograph and looked at it. He thought he knew now why it had been concealed, and perhaps the sad solution to the whole affair, but it gave him no satisfaction.

The day dragged on, the longest he could recall. Several times he was tempted to telephone Calvert, but resisted it until five o'clock. The superintendent answered immediately.

'I'm just sitting here on the end of the telephone. There's nothing much else I can do. I shall sleep for a week when this is over.'

'Any news?' asked Furnival.

'Everything seems to be going along nicely. Herring telephoned from Southampton a few minutes ago. Hunniker met his contact at the café, a young Mediterranean type gentleman carrying a cardboard carton. They got on the London train. Herring was about to follow them. Leslie and the Ape appear to be behaving normally, there's been no sign of Dinah Merriman.'

Furnival went up to the third floor and told Redmond the news, and together they shared a tin of sardines and an elderly fruit cake. Time dragged on. At seven o'clock he stood up to leave.

'Let me come with you,' begged Redmond. 'I may be some help.'

'No. Calvert and I and half-a-dozen coppers are going to be conspicuous enough.'

'I'll keep out of sight unless I'm needed. Please, Matthew, it's the least I can do.'

'Well, I'd rather you didn't, but I don't see how I can stop you. Don't approach Calvert or me, though.'

He went down to his own room, washed and changed, and left to pick up the car. It was seven-forty when he reached Alder Court, and the street was very quiet. He left his car and entered the Birdcage. Just inside the street door, at the foot of the stairs that led to Leslie's office, two young men were gossiping. One was the doorman who had taken his ten shillings the first time he had visited the club, and the other, he was almost sure, was one of his assailants. Neither of them glanced at him, and he slipped into the big club room.

It was almost empty. No more than thirty youngsters sat around the room. Loud beat music was playing but no one was dancing. The room was as dimly lit as usual.

Furnival sat down in the darkest corner and looked around him. He could not see

Leslie, the Ape, or anyone else on Leslie's staff. On the other hand he did not see anyone who could conceivably be a policeman.

At seven-fifty he was sweating with suspense. He was frightened to move from his seat to get a drink, or to draw attention to himself in any way. He glanced at the door and to his enormous relief saw Calvert coming in. The London superintendent looked as cool as ever, and perfectly at home in a long-jacketed suit and a flowered 'kipper' tie. He left the door ajar and circulated the room, waving airily to a few youngsters, then stopped beside Furnival and leant casually on the table.

'Keep your cool, man! You look ready for a firing squad!'

'Is everything all right?'

'Yes. Andreas and Hunniker are on their way. Leslie is somewhere on the premises. I've got two men out in the lane watching the back entrance, two in Alder Court, and three in here.'

'*In here?*' Furnival looked around. 'I don't see any.'

Calvert turned to face the room. 'Over there,' he said, 'black corduroy jacket and blue polo neck, see him? And there, ginger-haired bloke with a green shirt, and let me see, where is O'Mally? Oh yes, there, necking with that blonde. O'Mally takes his work very seriously.'

'Now there you really do excel us,' said Furnival admiringly. 'There isn't a single man in my division at Meddenham I could put down here who wouldn't stick out like a sore thumb.'

Calvert smiled. 'Include yourself. I'm drifting over to the door now to see if I can spot Hunniker coming in.' He moved back to the door and the three policemen he had indicated followed, O'Mally summarily dumping his blonde. Calvert kept his eye on the still open door, and after three or four minutes gave a curt nod and moved smartly out into the passage.

Furnival got to his feet quickly and followed the police. One or two of the youngsters in the room were now taking an interest in the general exodus.

On the stairs to Leslie's office Furnival

encountered two of Calvert's incognito constables. One had a competent forearm lock on the doorman of the Birdcage, the second young man, Furnival's assailant, lay in a crumpled heap at O'Mally's feet. O'Mally rubbed his knuckles, smiled sweetly at Furnival, and pointed silently up the stairs.

Furnival sped on up the stairs. The dim bulb still burned in the hall, but a crack of light now showed beneath one of the doors. He pushed it open, and stepped into a large, luxuriously furnished, and overcrowded office. He had a swift impression of deep carpets, a divan bed, a cocktail cabinet, a vast executive desk, and, in one corner, a battered old fruit machine, before he began to sort out faces. He made the eighth man in the room. At the far side of the room, behind the big desk, stood Mr. Leslie, flanked by the Ape and the lavender-suited young man who had enjoyed the National Gallery with Furnival. Just in front of the desk stood Hunniker, and a very bewildered dark young man who was presumably Andreas. Calvert and his ginger-haired constable were just inside the door. Alone on the top of the desk was a small cardboard carton, partly opened.

Calvert flicked a glance at the door and grinned at Furnival without for a moment taking his attention from Leslie and the Ape.

'Ah, here is Mr. Furnival,' he said. 'You owe him an apology, Mr. Leslie, for accusing him of breaking into your office.'

'Yeah, well, I'm sorry about that,' said Leslie. He had a light, girlish voice. 'I know who done it now, some of my boys seen him leaving. I'm not pressing charges, I took care of it myself.'

'Yes, very nasty,' murmured Calvert. 'You didn't quite kill him though.' He wandered across to the fruit machine and idly pulled on the lever. 'I wonder what he's going to tell us when he wakes up.'

'He won't tell you anything about my business. I run a decent, straightforward club where kids can enjoy themselves. You try to pin anything on me again and you're going to find yourself in big trouble, Superintendent. I got friends you know.'

'You're very welcome to them. In any case I didn't call in connection with your complaint.' He indicated the carton on the desk. 'Whose box is that?'

Leslie pointed at Andreas. 'It's his,' he said promptly.

Andreas jumped and turned a sickly ivory. 'No, yours, Mr. Leslie,' he shouted. 'I bring to you. Not mine, I only bring.'

Calvert beamed. 'Good lad,' he said. He turned back to Leslie. 'Finish opening it.'

'It's only peanuts,' said Leslie. 'You're making a bloody fool of yourself. It's tins of peanuts.'

Calvert nodded at the Ape. 'For our friend here? Open it.'

'You haven't got a warrant,' said Leslie desperately.

'I don't need one, the new Act, remember?'

Leslie picked up a small tack hammer from the floor where he had dropped it when Calvert entered, and finished breaking open the box. Then he slowly lifted out six tins one at a time, and set them on the desk. Calvert and Furnival took a step forward, they were sealed one-pound tins with keys attached to their lids, and their labels read, *Pyramid Giant Peanuts. Produce of Egypt.*

Calvert was reaching out to pick up a tin when Furnival heard the noise behind him. He spun round and saw the barman from downstairs charging through the door, a large crowbar raised above his head. Furnival and the ginger-haired constable leapt at the man, but he sidestepped Furnival and brought his crowbar down on the young constable's head, felling him instantly. After that all was confusion. Calvert jumped the barman and tried to prize the crowbar from his hand, meanwhile yelling, 'Watch Leslie! Don't let him get away!' Furnival thought he spotted Hunniker wrestling with Lavender Suit, and Andreas crouching terrified in a corner. Then Leslie dashed across the office swinging his hammer. Furnival blocked him and caught the hammer fairly painlessly on his shoulder, when eighteen stones of solid muscle landed on his back knocking him to the floor.

Furnival squirmed helpless beneath the Ape's weight as Leslie picked himself up and ran for the stairs. 'O'Mally will stop him,' he thought. But at that moment O'Mally himself lurched into view in the doorway locked in combat with Rob Redmond. Calvert put the barman down with a beautiful right cross and straightened up panting. 'Let him go, O'Mally, he's with us!' he shouted . . . 'For Christ's sake, get Leslie!' Then two huge hands fastened round Furnival's throat, there was a pounding of blood in his ears and behind his eyes, and everything started to go black. From out of the darkness there was a great reverberating crash and the Ape mercifully rolled off him.

Furnival looked up painfully through bloodshot eyes. A smoking service revolver hung at the end of Carl Hunniker's puny wrist.

19

Calvert stared at the gun as though a snake had suddenly reared its head.

'What did you bring that bloody cannon for? Give it to me.'

Hunniker handed it over without protest. 'I've never carried it before, sir. I just took it today to feel safer. Have I killed him?'

Calvert gave the Ape a cursory glance. 'No such luck.'

'I thought he was killing Mr. Furnival,' said Hunniker.

Furnival sat up and tenderly felt his throat. 'So did I,' he said.

'You all right?' asked Calvert.

'I think so.'

'*Where is Leslie?*' yelled the superintendent. 'Surely he couldn't have got past the lot of them? *O'Mally?*'

'I'm very sorry, sir, he rushed past me just as this bloke jumped me,' O'Mally glared at Redmond.

Redmond hung his head. 'I thought he was one of them, and he thought *I* was one of them,' he explained.

'Christ, you've got a genius for messing things up. See what you can do for the Ape and my chap here, and keep an eye on these three beauties. I'm going down to see what's happening. Come with me O'Mally.'

Furnival sat up against the wall and looked around him. The office was so littered with bodies it looked like the last act of *Hamlet*. The Ape, the barman, Lavender Suit, and the ginger-haired policeman were still prone. Hunniker and Redmond were kneeling beside the policeman. Andreas was still cowering in a corner. Furnival was amazed to see by the clock on the wall that it was barely half-past-eight. He got to his feet feeling shaky, walked across to the desk, and looked at the six peanut tins.

'God, I hope Leslie doesn't get away,' said Hunniker. 'He'll kill me for this.'

'I don't think so.' Furnival took up a position beside the door in case Andreas decided to make a break. 'He'll be thinking of his own skin now.'

'It had all gone so smoothly,' went on Hunniker. 'Andreas had just handed the stuff over when the superintendent burst in.'

'I expect they'll get them all,' but Furnival looked again at the clock, wondering what was keeping Calvert.

It was twenty minutes before they heard him on the stairs. As soon as he entered the room, Sergeant Pritchard and two constables at his heels, they knew the worst. His face was like thunder.

'You didn't get him?' ventured Redmond.

'No. Thanks solely to your efforts, Mr. Redmond, we didn't get him.' Calvert looked down at the bodies. 'Are they all fit to travel?'

'I think so.'

'Well, get them downstairs, constable. There's an ambulance waiting and a squad car for Andreas. As soon as they're sensible I want them all round at the station.'

The two policemen hauled Lavender Suit and the barman to their feet, and down the stairs. Two ambulance men came in, and with a great deal of effort, loaded the Ape on to a stretcher.

Calvert sat down at Leslie's desk and pulled out all the drawers. Furnival went over to him. 'What happened?' he said.

'I told you what happened. He got away. It was my fault as much as Redmond's. That barman was obviously lying doggo in the storeroom across the passage the whole time. He must have been, he didn't get up the stairs past O'Mally and Atkins. I should have checked it. Then when Leslie made his bolt it was real comic opera. Redmond was just charging up at the same moment, and O'Mally grabbed him. Leslie knocked over Atkins and the doorman he was restraining, and the doorman got away. Atkins and both my men in Alder Court chased him and Leslie but only managed to catch the doorman.' He savagely banged the contents of the desk drawers into a carton. 'Don't ask me why it took three of them to do it.'

'What about Leslie?'

'He 'disappeared'. Do your men ever give you that, Furnival? He just 'disappeared into thin air, sir!' The street was fairly crowded by then,' he added grudgingly.

'What about his car?'

'Still in the yard. Pritchard was out back with another of my chaps. They caught a bloke trying to get away in it. He was probably one of your attackers.'

'The other one was *hors de combat* on the stairs when I came up.'

'He still is unless the ambulance boys have scooped him up. When O'Mally puts them down they stay down.'

'We scooped him up,' put in Pritchard who had just reentered the office. 'Very nice little haul, sir. The Ape, Andreas, and five of Leslie's boys. Probably most of his mob.'

Calvert's glance withered him. 'Minnows! I wanted Leslie.'

'We'll get him. Where can he go? We've got his place at Richmond watched. You put a general call out to all cars.' Pritchard indicated Redmond and Hunniker. 'What about these two.'

'Take Hunniker down to the station. Mr. Redmond will make me very happy by going home. We'll take all this stuff from the desk with us, and load up that fruit machine.' Calvert looked round the rapidly emptying office. 'There's another team on the way, they should be here any time. They'll go over the place for hidey holes, and get the fingerprints.'

He looked at the peanut tins for the first time since he had re-entered the office.

'Well, there it is,' said Furnival.

'I certainly hope so.' Calvert touched one of the tins gingerly.

'Aren't you going to open it?'

'I'm almost scared to.' But he prized off the key and, steadying the tin, slowly opened it. Both men peered in. The tin was full to the brim with a white crystalline powder.

Calvert started to laugh, quietly at first, still staring down into the tin, then uproariously. He slapped Furnival on the shoulder.

'Christ, Furnival, suppose it had been peanuts!'

Furnival grinned. 'Not by specially escorted courier direct from the docks. Do you want me to come back with you?'

'No, go home and get some sleep. Come in and see me about eleven tomorrow, see what we've got by then. If only we'd got Leslie, my cup really would runneth over!'

Calvert locked the office door, and they went down to the street. All the activity was over. The police had emptied the dance hall and locked the whole place. One car still waited at the curb for Calvert.

He arranged the tins carefully on the back seat and got in. 'Where are you going to be tonight?'

'I think I'll go back to Avery Street. I'll keep a light in the window for Dinah! She might come back for the rest of her things.'

'Not that baby. You'll never see her again.' He lifted a hand. 'See you.'

Furnival recovered his car and drove slowly back to Avery Street. The reason he had given Calvert for going back there was not the whole, not even half, of the truth. He, too, was fairly sure that he would never see Dinah Merriman again. What he wanted, before he rejoined his family, was a last breathing space to worry out the wretched business of Barbara's murder.

He stopped at a bar on the way for a double whisky and a sandwich, and arrived at the house at ten-thirty. He went up to the second floor and looked in on Redmond. He found the young man at home, but not communicative. Dinah's room was dark and empty.

Furnival went down to his own room where he smoked and pondered until midnight, when he went to bed and, surprisingly quickly, fell asleep.

He woke at eight the next morning and had just finished dressing when there was a knock on the door. He opened it to Mrs. Marshall.

'Good morning, Mr. Furnival. Settled in all right, have you? I just brought you up a letter.'

Furnival took the letter from her in some surprise. So few people knew he was at the house and any of those would have telephoned had they wanted to contact him. He thanked Mrs. Marshall and closed the door. The envelope was light green and addressed in a flamboyant scrawl to Matthew Furnival. It was very fat. He sat down on the bed and opened it. Inside was a wad of several sheets of green notepaper, closely covered with the large handwriting, and one sheet folded separately. Furnival unfolded the single sheet.

'Dear Matthew,' he read, 'I'm very sorry I ran out on you and Rob the way I did. I hope you didn't get in trouble. I'm sending all I know about Mr. L. to Mr. Calvert. It honestly isn't much, but may help. You really are a very nice man. I can almost say — love — from Dinah.'

Furnival read the note through twice. For a moment he thought he smelled Dinah's haunting perfume in the room. He put the note away in his wallet, and skimmed quickly through the statement to Calvert. There was not a great deal of substance in it, the dancer had obviously been at pains to mind her own business, but it rang true. It could be valuable corroborative evidence.

He decided to visit Calvert as soon as he had breakfasted. It was just before ten o'clock when he arrived at his office.

Calvert was giving orders into two telephones simultaneously. He finished his conversations and nodded wearily at Furnival. 'You're early. Any news?'

Furnival laid Dinah's letter on the desk.

Calvert read it through. 'Good girl. Turned up trumps in the end. Was there a covering note?'

'Yes, but it wasn't of any consequence.'

'I'll bet it wasn't! Well, this will be quite useful together with the rest of what we've got.'

'Have you picked up Leslie?'

'No, we haven't. I can't understand it. I alerted the cars within five minutes of him leaving the club. I don't think he can possibly have got out of the area, but we've questioned every connection he's known to have in London, and turned over every place he might have gone to ground. So far nothing. The rest of the news is all good. The stuff in the tins was pure heroin, six pounds of it. With the black market price at three quid a grain that would mean big money after he'd adulterated it.

'All the boys talked,' he went on. 'We got plenty on the Blaikies, not only the drugs, but call girls and stolen cars as well. Enough to put them out of the way for a long time. We picked them up this morning, together with several hangers-on. We found the two hash-stuffed tyres your nephew accompanied from Liverpool. They were in a tyre depot, would you believe it?'

'How did Andreas get the heroin in?' asked Furnival.

'That was rather smart. He was a steward on an educational cruise ship. Not your dirty old tramp, but one of these liners that cruise the Mediterranean with reputable scholars aboard to lecture on classical remains. All quite ignorant of what was going on, of course, as was everyone else on the ship. Andreas seems to be a well-educated young man of good family, not the type whose movements they would watch too closely. His contact was a dancer in a closed circuit cabaret in Alexandria.'

'In a what?'

'Closed circuit cabaret. That's the sort of entertainment that even the city fathers of Alexandria wouldn't pass. They tour the Middle East playing to very rich and very dirty old men. English rose types are particularly popular. Anyway, Andreas got the stuff from this dancer, Interpol will take it from there. It was probably refined in the Lebanon and circulated with these cabarets.

'Leslie's scheme seems to have been very much as Hunniker told us. It was the second report of the Brain Committee in 1965 that put him on to it. This report, which was made necessary by the alarming increase in young addicts, made it illegal for general practitioners to prescribe heroin and cocaine to addicts. In future treatment was only to be carried out at special treatment centres which were to be given the right — by means of new legislation — to detain addicts compulsorily. Also there was to be compulsory notification of addicts to a central authority.

'The Dangerous Drugs Bill, when it came out in 1967, was not drastic — the vital compulsory detention clause had been dropped — but it seemed drastic to people with their moral fibre shot away. The offending permissive general practitioners forecast at the time that it would drive addicts to a large-scale imported black market.'

'Clever,' said Furnival, 'and vile.'

'Oh, Leslie was clever all right; and ruthless and decisive. But he should have held off while the heat was on. He should have postponed Andreas' visit while he knew we were watching him, but he has a reckless self-confidence that borders on insanity.' Calvert glared at the telephone. 'Where the hell can the bastard be?'

'What did your commander have to say?'

'He is 'delighted with my handling of the affair'. He thinks I have a bee in my bonnet over Leslie. He doesn't know what scum he is.'

The telephone rang. Calvert seized it, his eyes on Furnival. As he listened a look of surprise crossed his face. 'What?' he exclaimed. 'When? Well, when was he last seen? How could he get away, I thought he was — Yes, yes, I'll get on to it.' He replaced the receiver, frowning.

'A report about Leslie?' Furnival asked eagerly.

'What? No, it's Gino. The hospital has been on the line. He's disappeared. The nurse went in ten minutes ago and there was no sign of him. He could have been gone a couple of hours. I'd almost forgotten about him. I thought he was dying. I certainly assumed he was too ill to speak to me yet. I'll send a man to his home to see if he's there, although I'm very shorthanded. Finding him isn't really my concern.'

'Yes, it is,' said Furnival. He told Calvert why it was, and why he had not forgotten Gino.

The two of them went alone to Linden Terrace. Two large fit professionals must be enough to take one slight man who has been half beaten to death, even a man with spirit enough left to walk out of hospital. They were silent as they parked the car and crossed to the elegant little shop. It appeared to be deserted, the lights were out, and the sumptuous flower-piece in the window was beginning to fade.

'The boys haven't opened up this morning,' said Calvert. 'They must have lost their nerve after Saturday.' He tried the door. It opened, and the two policemen entered the salon. It looked much the same as usual, with the mirrors shining, and the myriad pretty bottles glinting in the gloom. There was the usual perfume on the air, but through it came another smell, a smell so horrible that Furnival shivered. A slight breeze from the open door stirred the satin curtains of the cubicles, and the one furthest from them lifted and came to rest on a large stylish suede shoe.

Furnival and Calvert looked at each other without a word. They walked down the salon and Calvert drew aside the curtain of the last cubicle. On his back on the floor lay what was just recognizable as Mr Leslie. A pair of long pointed scissors protruded from his chest. Every particle of skin had been burned from his face. On the floor beside him lay a pair of electric curling tongs, the scorched flesh still adhering to their blades. The stench was unbearable. Furnival turned away retching. Calvert said 'Gino?' He ran into the back room, and Furnival followed him.

Gino was seated at his desk. His throat beneath the battered face had been neatly cut. An old-fashioned open razor lay near his hand. He was quite dead.

Calvert turned to Furnival. 'He must have loved her very much.'

'She was his daughter,' said Furnival.

20

'Dinah Merriman had the answer,' went on Furnival. 'She said we should look for someone who loved Barbara. Only Gino loved her, and he loved her as a father, with possessive care.'

'You can't be sure,' said Calvert.

'Almost sure. Gino should have had her insurance card, that would have identified her, but he didn't produce it. And John said Gino had never employed a girl before, so why this girl? She was a very bad assistant, she could have sabotaged the business he was so proud of, but he kept her on, and 'wouldn't hear a word against her'. And somebody, probably Gino, made her a discreet allowance over and above her salary. Anyway, look at this,' Calvert took the old photograph from his wallet. 'I should have shown it to you before. I found it hidden away in Barbara's room. I think it was a treasured keepsake.'

Calvert looked at the photograph. 'Well, it wouldn't have meant anything if you had showed it to me. Who is it?'

'Surely it must be Barbara and her mother and brother. The picture looks nearly twenty years old. The face of the small boy haunted me. I was sure he was involved somewhere, and there were plenty of young men in the case, but I just couldn't place him. At one moment, I think it was in a dream, it suddenly came to me that it was Gino, but I rejected it. That child could not be more than twenty-three years old now and Gino must be forty.'

Calvert peered again into the child's faded features. 'It looks like Gino.'

'So like that it must be his son. I had never seen the actual boy, it was the likeness to Gino I recognized.'

'But I don't understand. Why did Gino keep the relationship a secret?'

'I suppose because he liked to appear a swinging young bachelor, a bit ambiguous sexually like his companions. To possess a rather dim, provincial, grown-up daughter, to say nothing of a son and a middle-aged wife, just wasn't his image. He'd probably left them in some dreary Northern town years before and half forgotten them. The strength of the feelings Barbara aroused in him must have amazed him.'

Calvert picked up Gino's telephone and called the murder squad and an ambulance.

'She was killed *because* she was in the wrong room,' he said when he had replaced the receiver.

'Exactly. It was as simple as that. Barbara was in her room, desperate for a fix and knowing Gerald was due to arrive next door. Her mind probably worked in just the way you said, here was that nice friendly Mr. Harrington who liked girls, he would give her the price of a fix. She wasn't thinking too clearly, as I say she was desperate, she undressed, slips on her wrap, and goes to Marian's room to wait for him.'

'And then Gino arrived.' Calvert took over. 'On a surprise visit to scold her in private, to tell her that she must pull herself together. But she isn't in her room, she is waiting, naked, in the room he has got for Harrington. There is a row, and, quite gently, he strangles her. He panics, and bolts just before Harrington arrives and Mrs. Corbett gets back to her post.'

'Why kill his daughter?' argued Furnival. 'Why not the man responsible?'

'Which man? The first one to seduce her? The one who got her pregnant? Who aborted her? The man who started her on dope? He couldn't kill half the human race, and that's whose victim Barbara was. But he did get Leslie. He didn't break out of hospital to escape his punishment. He had unfinished business to settle, and, by God, he settled it. It must have seemed like a miracle to him to find Leslie here on his own premises, as though he had been delivered to him. I don't see that he could possibly have sought him out in his condition.'

'I wonder why Leslie came here?' said Furnival.

'Why, it was safe. Gino was in hospital, it was Sunday evening, no one else would be here at least until this morning. And Leslie didn't have much choice, it had to be somewhere in this area.' They heard the other policemen descending to the shop. Calvert looked down at Gino's body. 'He saved me a tough decision, anyway,' he said. 'I would have hated prosecuting anybody for croaking Leslie!'

Suddenly Furnival had had enough. He wanted to put a lot of distance between himself and Leslie, and the Ape, and the almost ridiculous little man who had loved his daughter so much, but had not liked her enough to acknowledge her. He said goodbye to Calvert, pushed his way through the police who were crowding into the salon, and drove back to Avery Street. He hastily packed his belongings, said goodbye to Redmond, and drove on to the Harringtons' flat. Joanna and the Harringtons were all at home and he gave them a brief undetailed account of what had happened. That evening he visited Landseer, talked for a long time and got more than slightly drunk.

It was shortly before noon the following day when Calvert telephoned. Furnival finished locking his suitcase and took the receiver from Gerald.

'Ah, Furnival, you're still with us. I had the feeling yesterday that you would be leaving soon.'

'I would have been gone in ten minutes.'

'Then I'm glad I caught you. Just a couple of postscripts that might interest you. You were right about Gino and Barbara. We've been through his papers and found the marriage certificate and birth certificates, and family photographs. Also an address in Preston. The local police checked it for us this morning, but apparently Barbara's mother died just over a year ago, presumably shortly before the girl came to London. They haven't traced the brother yet.'

'All that colour and drama, and it was just a pathetic little family murder like so many of the rest,' said Furnival.

'I suppose so. But we cleared up a lot of colourful and dramatic vice on the way!'

'What will happen to Hunniker?'

'The commander is going to see what he can do for him at the embassy, or the military authorities, or whatever. Capturing undesirable criminals, smashing vice ring, saving the life of a high-ranking police officer! It shouldn't go too hard for him. He's hoping for a dishonourable discharge and parole. He didn't do the Ape any serious damage.

'There was just one other thing,' Calvert went on. 'One of my men stopped Dinah Merriman at London Airport early this morning. She was flying to Las Vegas — a lucrative engagement. I told him to let her go through, there was no real reason for me to hold her. It's hard to blame her. It's a short career, there's always someone younger and better on the way up.'

'Not better,' said Furnival. 'Not better.'

Calvert chuckled. 'She was really something, wasn't she? O.K. Someone younger on the way up. But then,' Furnival could visualize the eyebrow complacently raised, 'isn't there for all of us?'

He rang off. Elaine came out of the bedroom and kissed Furnival and Joanna fervently. 'Thank you a thousand times, darlings, for everything you've done. I can't think why Nicky isn't here to say goodbye, he promised faithfully that he would be. I'm beginning to be quite worried — '

Gerald seized the suitcase and hustled them firmly out of the flat. 'That goes for me too, old boy,' he said. 'I'll never be able to thank you enough for all your time and trouble, to say nothing of the danger you risked.' He stopped in the foyer and drew Furnival to one side. 'I'll tell you, Matt, I've had enough of wild oats and living it up,' he murmured. 'It was exciting and glamorous at first, keeping a mistress in a flat. Like a circus coming to town when you were a kid. But never again!'

Furnival solemnly shook hands with Gerald, and followed Joanna out to the car. He put the case in the boot, and had just got into the driving seat when the window of the Harringtons' flat opened and Elaine leaned out. Her voice came faintly fluting down. 'Wait, Matthew! Nicky is on the phone. There's been a little trouble with the police over his car. Would you be a darling and straighten it out? Matthew? . . . Matthew!'

'What is Elaine saying?' asked Joanna.

Furnival waved to Elaine, wound up the window, and pressed the starter. 'Just goodbye,' he said.

THE END

We do hope that you have enjoyed
reading this large print book.

Did you know that all of our titles
are available for purchase?

We publish a wide range of high
quality large print books including:
**Romances, Mysteries, Classics
General Fiction
Non Fiction and Westerns**

Special interest titles available in
large print are:
**The Little Oxford Dictionary
Music Book, Song Book
Hymn Book, Service Book**

Also available from us courtesy of
Oxford University Press:
**Young Readers' Dictionary
(large print edition)
Young Readers' Thesaurus
(large print edition)**

For further information or a free
brochure, please contact us at:
**Ulverscroft Large Print Books Ltd.,
The Green, Bradgate Road, Anstey,
Leicester, LE7 7FU, England.
Tel: (00 44) 0116 236 4325
Fax: (00 44) 0116 234 0205**